Sketches

A NOVEL

Doris B. Wolfe

HANNIBAL BOOKS
www.hannibalbooks.com

Scripture quotations taken from the NEW AMERICAN STANDARD
BIBLE®, Copyright ©1960, 1962, 1963, 1968, 1971, 1972, 1973, 1975,
1977, 1995 by The Lockman Foundation. Used by permission.
(www.Lockman.org)
Library of Congress Control Number: 2004115158
ISBN 0-929292-97-9

Verses one and three of "Jesus Loves Even Me",
words by Philip P. Bliss. Public Domain.
Verses one, three, and five of "How Firm a Foundation" from "K" in
Rippon's "Selection of Hymns," 1787. Public Domain.
Verse one of "Under His Wings" by William O. Cushing. Public Domain.
Verse three of "Like a River Glorious" by Frances R. Havergal.
Public Domain.
Verse two of "It Is Well with My Soul" by Horatio G. Spafford.
Public Domain.

**Special thanks
to**

Arthur, Bob, Charlene, Jeff, Kristin, Lorraine,
Martha, Neil, Ruth,
and Susan's and Kay's editorial teams
for proofreading and suggestions

ONE

Dani Austin snatched her pocket-sized, Portuguese-English dictionary from among the art supplies in her carry-on bag as the customs agent at the Belém airport frowned his disapproval at the delay. "Could you please repeat that, sir?"

The uniformed man rattled off an accented mixture of the two languages. Dani caught only the words "why" and "have." She had already opened both of her suitcases for him to inspect. Did he now want to see the contents of her large box?

A woman waiting three people back in line called out, "Would you like help in translating?" Before Dani could reply, the tall brunette smiled and spoke in Portuguese to the agent, who motioned her forward to serve as interpreter.

"He wants to know why you've brought so many art supplies to Brazil," she said.

"I'm an artist. I'll be drawing illustrations for primers for a mission organization," Dani replied.

"For how long?" was the next question.

"I have a one-year temporary visa."

"Where will you live?"

Dani pulled the address from her bag and showed the man. He nodded and gave the paper back. Then he asked the interpreter a few questions before waving them both on.

"You can re-lock your suitcases. We're both done," she told Dani. "Here, I'll help you put them on a cart."

The woman put her own luggage on a second cart. They both moved out of the area and headed toward the exit.

"I'm Rebecca Holman. Your mission is close to the international school where my husband and I work."

"I'm Daniela Austin."

"I suppose Kelcey will be waiting outside to take you to the mission center."

"Kelcey? I sent a fax to Mr. Roy Davis."

"Roy's in Brasilia. In fact, Kelcey's the only one at the center right now. Everyone else is in the capital for your mission's biennial conference."

"Oh, my. So Mr. Davis probably never received my fax."

"When did you send it?"

"Yesterday. I know that's short notice. But I was supposed to arrive the beginning of July. When I checked on my ticket a few days ago, I discovered the travel agent hadn't confirmed it and that the flight was filled. But she could get me a last-minute deal if I could get to Miami in time. She even took care of having the consulate adjust the date of my visa.

"My mom helped me pack in two days while my dad located a ticket for a connecting flight to Miami. Dad tried several times to fax Mr. Davis, but it didn't go through until just before I left home yesterday."

They exited the terminal into a crowd of people waiting for arriving friends and family members to clear customs.

Dani felt a sharp tug on the strap of her carry-on bag, which contained her newest sketchpads, as well as pastels, acrylics, brushes, and pencils—all means to her trade. She'd been afraid to put them in a suitcase in case it got lost. Now she grasped it with both hands before it could be stolen. She whirled to catch a glimpse of the would-be robber, but the young urchin sprinted around the corner of the building. *Close call*, she thought.

Dani moved to an open space on the sidewalk. She pushed a lock of damp, curly hair away from her face. Was Belém always this humid at 3 a.m.? How would she find this Kelcey person? What if he hadn't shown up? Would riding in a taxi be safe at this hour? How much would a taxi cost to the center? She didn't even know where it was situated in relation to the airport.

She watched from a distance as Rebecca Holman hugged a man and a girl. *Must be her family*, Dani thought. The girl took over wheeling the cart for her mother. They stopped by Dani.

"Daniela, this is my husband, John, and daughter, Kristy."

"Hello. I'm Daniela Austin."

"I just explained your situation to John. He hasn't seen either of your mission's vehicles waiting here. You're welcome to ride with us. We'd be happy to drop you off."

"But I have all this luggage."

"No problem," John assured her. "We brought a *Kombi*. We're parked up ahead by the curb."

Dani had no idea what a *Kombi* was, but if it was big enough for all of them plus the luggage, she'd prefer riding with them than in a taxi. "Thank you. That's nice of you to offer."

Kristy leaned against the handle to steer the cart down the sidewalk. "What did you bring me, Mom?"

Rebecca chuckled. "At least you waited two minutes before asking. I'm impressed. The list is too long to enumerate now. I'll unpack in the morning. But I guarantee you'll be pleased."

"How was the flight?" John stopped beside a red, box-shaped van and unlocked the back. He began sliding luggage in.

"Routine. I was tired enough to nap during much of it."

"Did you wear yourself out the last two-and-a-half weeks shopping for Kristy or caring for your parents?"

"Both. Dad improved rapidly after his surgery. I'm sure Mom will be able to cope with the rest of his recovery needs now."

"Good. Kristy and I will return these carts and be right back. You two can hop in."

Rebecca turned to Dani. "Your center and our school are in a suburb about 25 minutes away. You can share the middle seat with Kristy. My daughter can be quite inquisitive, so feel free to put a halt to her questions at any point."

"How old is she?"

"Nine."

As soon as the child snapped her seat belt, she asked, "What was your name?"

"Daniela Austin. My friends call me Dani, spelled D-A-N-I."

"Can I call you Dani?"

Rebecca looked over the front seat as John pulled out of the airport. "No. But maybe she'll let you call her Miss Dani."

Dani nodded. She was trying to view some of the scenery yet still listen to this family. Occasional street lamps illuminated a mixture of wooden shacks and old stucco-over-adobe houses. Some were painted bright colors; others were whitewashed or unpainted.

At a red light John pulled the *Kombi* into a left-turn lane and stopped. Across the street was a small airport.

"Another airport so close to the first one?" Dani asked.

"Júlio Cesar airport—it's for private planes," John replied. "Kelcey keeps your mission's plane at the Airclub hangar."

"He's a pilot? What type of plane does he fly?"

"A Cessna 206," Kristy broke in. "Six people fit in it. I wish Kelcey would take me for a ride."

The plane didn't sound very big. Not compared to the two jets she'd just flown in.

"Are you a teacher?" Kristy asked.

"No. I'm an artist."

"You paint pictures?"

"Yes. But I also draw with special pencils and pens. I'll be illustrating books for Indians so they can learn to read."

"Cool." Kristy now turned to her mother. "Can I stay up the rest of the night? I've never been up all night before."

"No, dear. You need to go to bed when we get home." At another traffic light, Rebecca pointed at a cement structure jutting into the sky. "Daniela, that is the *Entroncamento*, a landmark for this section. The road we're pulling onto is called BR-316, the main artery between Belém and Brasilia."

"Apparently no one received my fax. My arrival is unexpected. Maybe you should drop me off at a motel instead of going to the center in the middle of the night like this—if the motel accepts American dollars."

"Your center maintains an apartment for guests," Rebecca said. "If it's not available, we'll give you Kristy's bed. She'll sleep in a hammock until something else is arranged. Besides, you'll want to delete the word 'motel' from your vocabulary while you're in Brazil; only people with disreputable morals stay in one. Respectable folks stay in hotels."

Thankfully the van interior was too dark for them to see her blush. "I appreciate the offer. Your help is a blessing."

John turned off the highway onto a narrow, unpaved road with deep ruts and stopped before a large gate. "Here we are."

A uniformed night watchman stepped out of a tiny, adobe gatehouse. John rolled down the window. The two men conversed. The guard returned to the gatehouse and picked up a phone.

"He's phoning Kelcey," John explained.

"Cool!" Kristy exclaimed. "We get to see Kelcey."

"He may not be too happy to see you in the middle of the night, Kristy," John said wryly.

The watchman unlocked the padlock, swung the gate open, and directed them to drive to the guest apartment, where Kelcey would meet them. They passed a few buildings that looked like summer cottages one would find around any lake in the States. John drove into a driveway and turned off the engine.

A man rode up on a bicycle. Two loping German shepherds followed him. He wore jeans and a T-shirt. His auburn hair was mussed, as if he hadn't taken time to comb it. He yawned as he leaned the bike against the outside of the building.

Kristy opened the window beside her. "Kelcey! Mom's back from the States, and I got to stay up! But I have to wait till morning to see what she bought me."

"This is morning." The man smiled as he walked to the passenger side of the *Kombi*. "Welcome back, Rebecca. Hello, John and Kristy. What's this about a visitor?"

"Her name's Miss Dani," Kristy exclaimed. "Hi, Shadow and Sheba!"

"Let your mom talk," John murmured.

"I met Daniela Austin going through the customs line. She had sent a fax to Roy explaining her abrupt change in travel plans but didn't know everyone's in Brasilia." Rebecca glanced back. "Daniela, this is Keith Kelcey."

"Good to meet you," Dani said.

"Welcome to Belém, 'Gateway of the Amazon.' "

"Thank you. I'm glad to be here."

"Let's move your stuff into the apartment so the Holmans can head home and all of us can get some rest." He opened the side door of the vehicle but looked down at the animals. "Are you afraid of dogs, Daniela?"

"Only rottwielers, dobermans, and other attack dogs."

He grinned. "You're safe. Just don't tell any locals that Shadow and Sheba are quite the gentleman and lady. They're supposed to guard the center."

Dani stepped own. The gorgeous dogs looked her over; two black noses sniffed her proffered hand. When their tails wagged in acceptance, she scratched behind their ears.

John had the back of the vehicle open and showed Kelcey which luggage was Dani's. The two men carried the items to the apartment door. John returned to the van.

"Thank you again," Dani told the Holmans.

"See you later!" Kristy called from the departing *Kombi.*

Keith Kelcey tried several keys from a huge key ring before he found the right one. He unlocked the door, flipped the light switch, and carried in the luggage.

Dani followed him. The apartment was small but nice. The front room served as a combination kitchen/living/dining room. To the left were the bathroom and bedroom. Plain, white curtains hung at the screened windows—windows sporting metal security bars as if this were a jail.

The pilot laid a key to the apartment on the table and walked over to the dresser in the bedroom. He immediately turned on a circular fan to the highest setting and pushed a knob on the top to make it rotate back and forth. "You'll want this on all night to keep mosquitoes off you."

Dani kicked off her sandals and let the cool linoleum floor soothe her bare feet, which now were swollen from traveling. She set her canvas bag on top of the wooden table. The adrenaline had faded. She was wilting fast in the heat and humidity.

He rejoined her by the table. She noted that his eyes were the most marvelous hazel color she'd ever seen. She guessed he was about six-foot-three, 180 pounds, and around 27 or 28—the same age as her oldest brother. But she could tell by his expression that he considered her just a kid. Looking younger than her age had always been a problem.

"Which family are you visiting this summer?"

Her brown eyes widened with surprise. Which family? Summer? What was he talking about? "I'm here to work. I have a temporary visa good for one year. The Holmans mentioned you're a pilot. Do you fly often?"

"Twenty-five to 30 hours a month. But I do my own maintenance, paperwork, and P.R., which rack up my work hours. I'm also called on from time to time to fix washing machines, motorcycles, the group cars, etcetera."

"Must be nice to be so handy. I can barely screw in a light bulb."

"Your mechanical abilities can't be that limited."

"You'd be amazed. This conference everyone but you is attending—how long does it last? And why did you stay behind?"

"Ten days, which are almost halfway over already. Someone from each of our mission centers stays home to keep watch, so it's not left unoccupied. This year Roy Davis asked me to keep an eye on the place, which worked out well since I needed to do some maintenance on the plane before my next flight. Gilda, the Brazilian secretary, works in the office during the day. She and a gate guard keep tabs on things when I'm at the airport."

"Your wife went to Brasilia, too?"

"I'm not married."

"Oh." Instinctively she knew she was safe with him, but they had the matter of appearances to deal with. She might look naïve, but she was quite aware of how easily some people started gossip. "So, should I have accepted the Holmans' offer of Kristy's bed instead of staying here?"

"You're fine here for the time being. I'll phone Roy in a few hours and get further instructions. We'll find some *jeito*."

"*ZHEY-too?*" She struggled to pronounce the strange word.

"*J-E-I-T-O*. A very useful word which basically means 'skill.' You'll hear people use it often in many contexts. Some skillful solution—a way to do the impossible. That's the end of your first Portuguese lesson. He moved toward the bathroom and peeked in. "Your shower has an electric showerhead, which I doubt you've ever seen. You can adjust the temperature from hot to warm to cold, but don't touch the wires sticking out of the top."

"As in, don't get electrocuted?"

"You've got it. You'll soon discover the fan and shower are your best friends. You may even take several showers a day just to cool down. The water on the center is filtered and is safe to drink."

"Thanks. You've been very helpful."

He turned to leave but pivoted back when she spoke.

"One more question. You've turned on the fan to keep away mosquitoes—are they malarial?"

"Not in this section of Belém. In some of the Indian villages translators and literacy workers are exposed to malaria. But don't worry about it here. Try to get some sleep, Daniela. I'm sure you've had a long day. Be sure to lock your door."

"I will. Good night."

"Pleasant dreams." Keith rode off on his bike.

She locked the door and slid the curtains across the rods to close them. As she did, she again noted the bars. She was so tired and hot. If she could just manage not to touch the wires when she adjusted the water temperature on the showerhead, a shower would feel absolutely wonderful before she slipped into her bed.

Lord, what have I gotten myself into? No, she must not doubt. God had clearly led her to this place. *Please help me get used to Belém and be of value to the mission. Thank You for bringing me—and my art supplies—here safely. Now, could You please keep me from getting fried when I take this shower?*

TWO

Where was she? Keith knocked again and called her name. She couldn't be that heavy a sleeper. He peeked through the open curtains; the apartment was empty. He pulled out an extra key, unlocked the door, and dumped the grocery bags on the table.

He was responsible for the kid. So where had she gone while he was out buying breakfast? Did she have enough sense to stay on the center, or had she wandered out the gate?

When he'd spoken with Roy Davis on the phone an hour ago about being totally uninformed of the newcomer, the center director merely chuckled and said, "You need to get your head out of the clouds and listen to the grapevine more." Maybe so, but that didn't change the fact that he was stuck taking care of a kid who didn't know beans about living in Brazil. He wasn't even sure why she was here. Roy had been in a hurry to get to another meeting, so the conversation was cut short before he had a chance to ask.

Keith stepped outside and relocked the apartment. He got on his bike and circled the complex.

She was sitting on the Tatums' porch, bent over a pad of paper and scribbling with a pencil. Shadow and Sheba lay at her feet. When Shadow turned his head toward Keith, Dani looked up.

"Oh, hi."

He tamped down his irritation. "Hi, yourself. What are you doing?"

"They've been cooperative and have hardly moved, almost like they're posing for me."

What was she talking about? He looked over her shoulder. "Wow! You've captured their expressions perfectly. Drawing is your hobby?"

"Hobby? Are you joking? Mr. Pilot, you are looking at my vocation. I'm an artist."

He suddenly looked at her in a new light. Maybe she was out of high school after all. "Do you draw people, too?"

"You name it; I'll sketch it. That's why I'm here."

"I had no idea. Roy didn't mention your profession. Do you have other pictures in your book?"

"A few." She handed it to him.

He flipped through the first few pages. "You're good. Think you could sketch the plane sometime?"

"If you take me to the airport. I don't know what a Cessna 206 looks like. But if I see it, I can draw it."

"I bought some groceries to make breakfast. Not much, but it's the average Brazilian fare. I used the extra key to get in and left the bags on your kitchen table."

"Umm. I am hungry." She closed the sketchpad and stood.

"I thought you'd still be asleep after your late arrival."

"Too many new noises hitting my eardrums. I decided to explore a bit and ran into these cute subjects who just begged me to sketch them."

He pushed the bicycle as he walked beside her. "Begged, uh-huh, but not to be drawn. They wanted food."

"Little you know."

She was the greenhorn, not him, but he'd set her straight with a smile. "I have to feed them their breakfast soon. They sleep it off by nighttime when they go on guard duty."

She unlocked her door and set her pad and pencil down next to the plastic bags. She peeked at the items he'd purchased: little crusted buns, a jar of jelly, a can of powdered milk, a small jar of coffee, and a small sack of sugar.

"Thanks so much, Keith. What do I owe you?"

"Four thousand *cruzados*."

"Four thousand—" She made a choking sound.

"If you want to exchange some dollars, we can do it today."

"Would you like to join me for a cup of coffee and explain why I owe 4,000 whatever-it-is for this meager amount of groceries?" She set the teakettle on the gas stove and opened a cupboard to look for dishes.

He chuckled, turned a chair around, and straddled it so he could watch her. "I take it you didn't do your homework and learn about our currency and the present exchange rate?" He watched her eyes spark at his tone.

"Guilty as charged. But I'm not so dumb that I don't know each country has its own currency."

"Right now the Brazilians use *cruzados*, but we hear talk of dropping some zeros and changing its name, so don't get too used to it.

"I spoke with Roy about an hour ago. He suggested I ask the Holmans if Kristy could stay with you each night as a companion and—sort of—chaperone."

"A . . . chaperone." Dani set two mugs and spoons on the table.

"Kristy asks lots of questions but should tire out no later than 10 p.m., so you'd have peace the rest of the evening."

"Who says I stay up later than 10? And where would I put her? This apartment has only one single bed." She poured hot water into the mugs.

"See those hammock hooks in the wall? Kristy would bring one to sleep in. Call it a Brazilian-style sleeping bag."

"How strange. But I'm willing to give it a try. I didn't know what those hook things were." She took her place at the table.

"I found out what happened to your fax."

She cocked her head and waited for him to explain.

"Gilda saw it was for Roy and re-faxed it to him in Brasilia. But he was in meetings and didn't even see it until early this morning."

Dani sighed. "I'm glad God sent the Holmans to help me."

"Yes. Let's pray before we eat. After breakfast I'll take you on a tour of the center."

A half-hour later, Keith ushered her into the center's office building. "Daniela, this is our secretary, Gilda Dias. She usually works mornings only, typing and answering the phone, but during the conference she works all day. Her husband teaches at a local seminary."

He completed the introduction in Portuguese. Gilda smiled sweetly and said a few words of welcome, which he translated. Dani returned the smile.

When they were once again outside, Dani asked, "Why does everyone call you Kelcey?"

"My last name seems easier for Brazilians to pronounce. Almost all of my friends and co-workers picked up on that phenomenon. You can call me that, too, if you'd like."

"I'd prefer calling you Keith. Unless you purposely keep using my formal name in retaliation." She didn't wait for his reply. "The center is larger and has more buildings than I expected."

"We serve 10 translation teams, although two are on furlough and two are doing group duty in Brasilia this year. Here's the old hangar and airstrip, which was shut down years ago when the city grew up around us. Now we hangar the Cessna at Júlio Cesar. The walled section beyond the strip is a wealthy subdivision. Beyond it is A.I.S. property—Amazon International School—where we're headed next. This well-worn path along the back wall leads to the school. So far we've felt safe walking it alone in the daytime, but don't try it at night."

"Your statements concerning security precautions aren't just to scare me, I assume?"

He shook his head. "Afraid not. Poverty is widespread; therefore, so is thievery. Back to what I was saying about the school. A.I.S. is accredited for kindergarten through 12th grade. Since this is the middle of June, school isn't in session. Here's the Holmans' house."

Rebecca Holman was in the kitchen making cookies. She invited them to sample a few, along with some fruit juice. She slid another cookie sheet into the oven. "I can guess why you're here. Roy phoned earlier and asked if Kristy could spend the next few nights at Dani's apartment. She can bring her hammock. We said, 'Sure.' John and I will walk her over after supper."

"Thanks. Better give us until 9 o'clock," Keith said. "We'll be in town for supper tonight." He watched Daniela blink at his pronouncement, but she didn't challenge him until they walked home.

"So, what is the plan for the rest of the day?" she asked.

"I'll drop off a couple of sandwiches for your lunch. I need to make a quick trip to the airport and talk to Bentes about using his hangar to work on the plane tomorrow. At 2 o'clock we'll head into town, exchange some money for you, and start the process of registering you with the Federal Police."

She stopped walking. "Registering me for what?"

"Standard procedure. Don't worry. All of us must register our presence in this country and get an I.D. card. Be sure to bring your passport, as well as whatever dollars you want to exchange. We might finish this afternoon, if we're lucky. Then we'll see some of Belém and eat out."

"If we're lucky?"

"If not, the process could carry over into another day."

"I'm sorry you have to go to all this trouble for me."

"No problem. At least you don't have to put up with my cooking."

"That bad, huh?"

He patted his flat stomach. "I'm not dying of malnutrition yet, but I won't win any blue ribbons either. Actually a Brazilian woman works for me two afternoons a week and cooks my suppers for those nights. But this isn't one of them, so we'll go out."

Dani tackled the mundane task of unpacking. With a limited wardrobe of mix-and-match items, she didn't take long to put everything away. By the time she finished eating the sandwich and banana Keith had left, she felt wilted from the heat and humidity. A cool shower would feel marvelous. And maybe if she washed her curly brown hair, it wouldn't look like such a mess. She was very careful not to touch the showerhead wires.

What did one wear to a police station in a foreign country? Not that she had many choices. She picked out a lemon-colored, cotton-knit dress and pulled it on. Then she draped a dry towel over her pillow, lay across the bed with the fan blowing on high aiming straight at her, and promptly fell asleep.

Someone was calling her. Groggily she stood and smoothed out the dress. Keith was at the door.

He grinned. "Been sleeping? Take a look in the mirror."

She turned on the bathroom light and groaned. Her hair looked worse than before she'd showered. She plastered it down with tap water and ran a wide-toothed comb through the mop. "This I.D. card I have to get—will they put my picture on it?"

"Uh-huh." Keith's eyes twinkled.

"No one told me it would be this humid here. I look awful."

"Your hair isn't too bad. Actually, it's kind of cute."

She rolled her eyes in disgust.

"No one ever looks good for I.D. cards or passport photos or drivers' licenses. Are you ready? We need to get going."

"Sure." She slipped on a pair of sandals, grabbed a sketch-pad, and stuffed two pencils and a gummed eraser into her shoulder bag.

"Why are you bringing that stuff?"

She shrugged. "Might see something I want to draw. I never go anywhere without some supplies."

A red sports car was parked in the drive. Keith opened the passenger door for her.

She slipped into the bucket seat. "Is this yours?"

"Don't I wish! This is just a group car we can use for a small fee."

"Pretty snazzy for missionaries."

"The old vehicle was a station wagon, but when it died a couple of months ago, the dealer didn't have another station wagon in stock. So we ended up with this *Gol*."

"What a pity."

Keith laughed and shifted gears as they passed through the gate. "I drive it whenever I can." The car bumped down the dusty road to BR-316. Once on the main road, Keith pointed out the grocery, a bakery, a Baptist church and seminary, and a new mall under construction.

Traffic was heavy. The six-lane road widened into four sets of two lanes each, with two sets going each direction.

"These middle lanes are called express lanes," Keith said as they whizzed past the slower traffic, which included buses of various colors. "Anyone who's going as far as the bus station can use them. As you can see, a curb keeps us from being able to exit until then."

"Why are the buses different colors?"

"Each color is owned by a different company. The kind you'll take from the center to town is the yellow *Forte*. But don't do it alone the first few times. Only certain *Fortes* leave the center of town and go all the way past our center; the others turn at the *Entroncamento*. You'd end up lost."

"I don't know if I'll ever be adventuresome, or proficient in Portuguese, enough to ride a bus to town and back."

"Mind if I ask you something?"

"Go ahead. But I might not answer."

"Artists are supposedly temperamental. Are you?"

"I can be a bear. But I've heard people with reddish hair get angry easily, too. Does it hold true for auburn as well?"

"Possibly," he admitted. "The jungle-looking area on our right is the *Bosque*, which covers a whole square block, and blocks are long in Belém. Can I ask you another something?"

"Well, I don't know. One question per hour is probably more than enough for me to handle."

He chuckled. "Dani, you're a strange mixture of wisdom and naïveté. Just how old are you? And, yes, I know I should never ask a woman her age, but I'm breaking the rules."

"I won't even ask how old you think I am. Believe it or not, I'm 20. And I'd guess you're 27 or 28."

"Good guess. I'll be 28 next month. On our left is the bus station."

"I don't see any yellow buses in there."

"Because it's for the long-distance buses, not the city buses."

The divided lanes ended; the eight lanes merged to six, three in each direction. She counted five vehicles side by side, all traveling their same direction.

"Don't they believe in these painted lanes?"

"Nope. This is a neighborhood market area. Lots of congestion here."

"Is it always this bad?"

"Except Sunday mornings and in the middle of the night."

How could he be so cheerful about it? She bit her lower lip and resolved not to distract him with more questions. They moved onto a wide, one-way, tree-lined avenue, but four or five cars, buses, and trucks were still squeezed into three lanes.

"Mango trees," Keith indicated with a thrust of his chin. "As well as being 'Gateway to the Amazon', Belém is the 'City of Mango Trees.'"

The immense shade trees lined both sides of the avenue the rest of the way into town. Keith pointed out the zoo, which also filled a whole square block. "We'll go there Sunday afternoon," he promised. "The zoo is a 'must see' for newcomers."

Keith parked the car near the banking district and led her to an old building, where he handled the exchange of $200 into *cruzados*. When they walked out of the building, Dani asked, "Why didn't we go into one of the banks?"

"He gives us a better deal. Be sure to hold on to your bag with a tight grip. Foreigners are a prime target for robbery. I'd hate for you to lose your wad of money."

"A wad is right. I almost feel rich. Maybe I should hire an armed guard."

"Next stop is a one-hour photo shop for your 'mug shots.'" He drove to the main street, *Presidente Vargas*, and found another parking spot. An urchin ran up and spoke. Keith nodded.

"What was that all about?"

"He's going to 'guard' the car for us. I'll pay him a hundred *cruzados* for the service." When she cocked her head he added, "A small price for insuring the tires will still have air and hubcaps when we return."

"You mean if you don't 'hire' him, he'll steal the hubcaps or let air out of the tires?"

"Uh-huh."

Dani tried to absorb all the sights and sounds as they walked. She hadn't realized she was distracted until Keith put his hand on her waist and pulled her close, her shoulder bag swinging against him. "Oh!"

"Don't slug me. I'm just protecting you and your money," he said. "You're so absorbed in looking around, you didn't notice the urchins tailing us and eyeing you."

"I'll be more careful. You can let go of me."

He glanced over his shoulder before he released her. "They ducked around the corner."

Her heartbeat slowed to almost normal. But she did keep a tighter grip on her bag.

At the photo studio, she paid the photographer the price Keith stated, ran a comb through her unruly locks, and smiled for the picture.

"We've got an hour to kill before the photos will be ready," Keith said. "Let's meander through some souvenir shops."

Dani was entranced with the butterfly-wing pictures and trays. She picked up a round frame with the map of Brazil made from Blue Morpho wings. "I'd love to have this." She flipped it over to see the price and calculated the exchange. "Not bad. I can afford this."

She paid the cashier, who wrapped the item in newspaper.

"Thirsty yet?" Keith asked. "I could use a soft drink."

"Sure. Sounds good."

He led her to a table at Bos's, ordered soft drinks, and glanced at his large watch. "Almost time to pick up the photos."

"What kind of watch is that?"

"A chronograph. As well as being a regular watch, it has a stopwatch so I can keep track of my flight time."

"Pretty fancy."

"But a necessity in my line of work."

After picking up the set of four photos, they drove to the Federal Police station, a non-impressive building several stories high. A guard checked Keith's I.D. and her passport and allowed them to climb the dimly-lit stairs to the second story.

They entered the first office on the left and took chairs against the wall until a young man motioned for them to approach his desk. Keith spoke to him in Portuguese.

The young man examined Dani's passport. He looked at her to compare the picture with reality. Handing over a sheaf of papers, he fired off instructions and gestured toward the door.

"We may finish in an hour," Keith mumbled as he sat down beside her, "or we may have to return Monday to finish, since it's almost 4 o'clock." He took a pen from his shirt pocket and began translating the questions. He filled in the forms with her replies.

Dani gave an exasperated sigh. "Why do they need to know my parents' birthplaces, address, and occupations? I'm the one here."

"Your guess is as good as mine. Background check? Have any deep dark secrets they're going to uncover?"

"You think I'd tell you?"

"Confession is good for the soul."

She leaned closer and tapped the paper. "Write, scribe."

When he completed the last blank, Keith said, "Now for fingerprinting—down the hall in another room."

"Fingerprinting? As if I'm a criminal?"

"Standard procedure."

Maybe so, but when the guy inking Dani's 10 fingertips and pressing them onto a card gave her some rather bold, non-standard glances, she was glad Keith was in the same room to defend her if necessary. Then back to the original office to show all the papers to the first man.

"Sit tight," Keith instructed, "while I run down to the corner bank to pay the fees."

"The bank? Can't you just pay it here?"

"This is Brazil. They do it differently." He stated a price. She pulled the *cruzados* from her bag. "Whatever you do, don't move from this room."

"Yes, sir." She opened her sketchpad and began to doodle. A moment later she realized she was sketching Keith's profile.

Nope. Better not. She flipped to the next sheet and sketched the young man at the desk.

Keith dashed in at one minute until five with the payment receipt. He managed to persuade the official to type out Dani's temporary I.D. card even though it meant a few minutes of overtime.

When the man presented it to her, she signed the sketch, tore it from the pad, and handed it to him with a smile. "Thank you." She hoped he understood.

Duly surprised and impressed at the likeness, the worker looked her over again before mumbling a word she assumed was the Portuguese "thank you."

Keith put his hand on her elbow. They walked down the stairs. "You made a friend back there."

"Think so? I just did it on a whim."

"Still, he liked the drawing. Sure doesn't hurt our mission to have some friends in this building. Your real card will be ready in three or four weeks, after the paperwork is processed in Brasilia, so we'll be back here again. Actually I'm surprised we finished so fast. I got a break at the bank—not too many people in line, for once."

They stepped out into the bright sunshine and heard a screech of tires, followed by the sickening thud of a taxi hitting a pedestrian about 50 feet away.

Holding her breath, Dani stood gaping, rooted to the sidewalk.

The driver sped off as people thronged to help the victim. But at the next intersection, cars blocked the taxi's escape.

"Let's get out of here." Keith grabbed Dani around the shoulders and propelled her away from the crowd.

"Where are we going? The car's over there."

"Too close to the mob. We can't get near it now. This calls for a long walk around the block—or even a couple of blocks— until things settle down." He steered her around the nearest corner.

Ten steps and Dani started to shiver, even though the temperature was 95 degrees in the shade. She dragged her feet somewhat, but Keith kept her moving. "What's going to happen?"

His arm around her tightened. "Don't ask, Dani. This isn't the States. Justice takes a different form here. Believe me, you don't want to know."

THREE

"What happened then?" Kristy asked from her hammock as Dani adjusted the fan, making it rotate and blow on both of them.

"Hum? Oh, after we ate steak at *La en Casa*? Well, we walked to the main plaza—"

"*Praça*."

"*PRAH-sah*," Dani tried to pronounce it correctly, "and he pointed out First Baptist Church and the pink theater."

"The *Teatro da Paz*."

Dani'd had enough of Portuguese. "And he said the Peace Theater is a work of art. He told me I'd have to see the inside of it someday."

"I think it's ugly."

Smiling, Dani put one hand on the light switch but gasped as she spotted an eight-inch lizard stretched across the window screen. Was it on the inside or the outside?

"What's wrong?" Kristy sat up in the hammock. "Oh, cool."

She ran to the window and flicked her fingers against the screen. The lizard flew into the darkness while she put her ear to the window to listen. "Did you hear it go thud, Miss Dani? I think that's fun!"

"Did it hurt the lizard?"

"Naw. It'll be fine. Maybe just dazed a bit."

"I think you'd better climb back into the hammock now and go to sleep, Kristy."

She complied only with the first part of the request. "Did he kiss you good night?"

Dani rolled her eyes. Was this what it would be like to have a younger sister? Had she bugged her older brothers with such questions? "You and your parents were waiting here when we arrived. Did you see him kiss me?" She snapped off the light and padded to bed.

"No, but he could have kissed you downtown. Or in the car."

"I've known Keith less than 24 hours. He's only a friend. Besides, he thinks I'm just a kid."

"You don't look like a kid to me, so why would Kelcey think so? Did you know he's gone out with Miss Maggie Paige? I bet he's kissed her!"

Was she supposed to know Miss Paige? If she was someone famous, Dani couldn't place her. "Who's she?"

"My teacher. I've seen him walk her home sometimes." After a slight pause, Kristy added, "But usually Kelcey sticks to flying R.C.'s or playing volleyball with the guys."

Dani hated to show even more of her ignorance to a nine-year-old; however she swallowed her pride. "What are R.C.'s?"

"Radio-controlled airplanes. Lots of the guys and some of the adults buy kits from the States and make their own planes. Kelcey's made several. You've got to see them. Everyone watches when they fly over the soccer field at school or the old airstrip. Once Kelcey even let me take the controls, just for a minute or two. I didn't crash like Tommy said I would. I showed him. I think I'll get to fly again soon. Kelcey won't mind letting me."

The hammock creaked slightly. "Are you sure you'll be comfortable in that thing?"

"Thing? Oh, the hammock? I love sleeping in it."

Dani slid between the sheets and tried to pretend they were crisp and cool instead of warm and humid. It didn't work, but the bed felt good anyway to her tired, culture-shocked body. She'd had enough of Belém for one day.

If she listened carefully each night, she could learn a lot from this child. But she was so exhausted, she fell asleep while Kristy was still talking.

When Dani opened her eyes at 8 a.m., Kristy was already up and handed Dani a note before she could even get out of bed.

"Kelcey gave it to me for you," she divulged in an I-told-you-so tone. "He brought you more bread."

Dani scanned the note. *Went to Júlio Cesar. Rebecca will take you to the grocery at 10. She invited us for supper tonight.*

"Kristy, I'll be dressed in a few minutes. Would you like some bread and jelly for breakfast?" Dani headed for the bathroom.

"Today is pancake day. I think I'll go home. But can I watch you draw later?"

"I suppose. Shall I walk you home?"

"Naw. I'll be fine. I'm not afraid. I can run fast."

"You're sure?"

"Yeah. Mom says I just have to watch out for strangers when I walk here during the day. If I see any, I'm supposed to scream and run for the nearest house."

"I'd feel better if I walked you home."

But when Dani exited the bathroom five minutes later, Kristy had left.

The child returned later, tagged along as Dani drew, and asked countless questions. Dani breathed a sigh of relief when Rebecca arrived and sent Kristy home to clean her room while she and Dani went to the store.

The grocery was small and crowded. Unable to understand the labels on everything, Dani felt like a two-year-old needing constant supervision. Rebecca patiently translated for her as they navigated the aisles. The veteran made suggestions as to which brands were better. Dani put them in her basket. The checkout line was another hassle. Dani felt totally worn out by the time Rebecca dropped her off at the apartment. Two hours to buy groceries for one person for the next week! She hoped every week wasn't this tiresome.

That evening Keith walked her over to the Holmans'. They chatted with John, Rebecca, and Kristy for a few minutes before two more guests arrived.

Kristy jumped up and down. "Miss Maggie! I caught a lizard and put him in a jar. Wanna see?"

"Whoa," her father stated. "Introductions first." He turned to his wife.

Rebecca introduced Dani to Maggie Paige, Kristy's teacher, and to Ruth Larsen, the school bookkeeper. Maggie was in her 20's, with long, blonde hair and gorgeous blue eyes. Ruth was probably in her 40's, with salt-and-pepper hair. Both women welcomed Dani to Belém. Then Kristy led her laughing teacher off to her room.

The pizza supper was a success. Rebecca served five large pizzas with various toppings. Keith amazed Dani with how much he ate.

She covertly watched Maggie and Keith. She did sense some spark between them, which was better to know right from the start. Dani had felt a definite attraction to the handsome pilot. But to him she was just a little sister to show around and tolerate until the others returned from the conference. She needed to cool her feelings immediately.

After the women washed and dried the dishes, the group played a few table games. Kristy chose Pictionary to play first. "Dani's on my team," she announced smugly.

"No fair," Keith protested. "She's a pro. I suggest she draws left-handed so the rest of us stand a chance."

"I second the motion," said Rebecca.

So Dani complied. Her team still won.

They played several other games before Kristy started yawning.

"Time to say good night," Dani observed aloud. Keith seemed a little reluctant to leave, so she quickly added, "No need for you to walk with us. Kristy can make sure I don't get lost."

Keith stood, though, and accompanied Dani to the door while Kristy grabbed a few things from her room. "If you'd like to try church tomorrow, I leave at quarter till 9. You won't understand much, but you're welcome to join me if you'd like to leave the center for a while."

"In the *Gol*?" When he grinned and nodded, she said, "Sure. See you then."

She was punctual. Keith appreciated not having to wait for her to apply makeup or whatever girls normally took so long to do. As he drove to church, he told Dani what to expect.

"I attend a multi-cultural, evangelical church. We have members from Japan, France, Spain, Mozambique, Canada, the States, and, of course, Brazil. The words to hymns and choruses are projected onto a screen, but often you'll hear some people around you singing in their own language at the same time others sing in Portuguese. I think it's exciting because it helps me visualize how people from every tribe and nation will be in heaven praising the Lord. Imagine hundreds of thousands of people gathered before His throne worshiping Him in various languages and styles."

"Sounds like Revelation."

"Exactly."

"No express lanes today?" Dani asked as Keith chose the slower lanes along with the buses.

"We're not going as far as we did the other day. The church is on a side street just after the *passarela*."

"The what?"

"The fenced-in passenger bridge over the eight lanes of traffic. You probably didn't give it much thought Friday when we drove under it. I should mention that I teach the juniors' Sunday-school class."

"I didn't think about Sunday school. What should I do while you're teaching? I mean, if I go to one of the adult classes, I hope no one asks me a question. I don't think I can get past *Bom dia*."

"You can join me in the junior class. We don't use big words."

"I wouldn't even recognize small words."

He grinned. "The kids would love having you draw something in that sketchpad you couldn't leave behind."

"Hey, don't knock my security blanket. I could illustrate whatever story you're teaching. If I can figure out what you're saying."

"Today I'm teaching from Acts 9, about Saul's conversion."

"Hmmm. I can draw that."

Keith introduced Dani to his 11 students representing four nationalities: Brazilian, Japanese, American, and Canadian. They were curious but finally turned their attention to him when Dani took a seat at the back of the room.

Thank you, Dani, for realizing you're a distraction to the kids if you're within their line of vision, he thought.

He spoke to the kids in Portuguese. He glanced occasionally at Dani. Her hand moved rapidly. Rarely did she use the eraser. When he finished the story, she nodded. She was done already? He invited her to show it to the children, whose reaction mirrored his own: awe and curiosity. How could she make the people look so alive? And in such a short time?

After he taught the memory verse, the kids begged him to let them play Uno. He glanced at Dani, who arched her eyebrows. "Playing a game helps them get to know each other. They love it," he explained. "You could learn some numbers."

"Oh, really?"

He could tell she was trying to hide a smile. But by the time the class ended, Dani could count to 10 and had picked up some other simple words.

The sanctuary was crowded. Keith found room for them and smiled a greeting to the people around. The music began, a teen turned on the overhead projector, and the words to the first song appeared on the screen. He tried to concentrate on the meaning but wondered how Dani would deal with hearing so many foreign words. By the end of the third song she began to fidget and looked unfocused. He'd probably done the same a few years ago when he first arrived in Belém.

The pastor announced the Bible reading. Keith leaned over and whispered, "Isaiah 53."

Dani found the page in her English Bible. She fiddled with the pencil in her hand but didn't open the sketchpad—although she appeared tempted.

The closing hymn was familiar. He watched her brighten and heard her singing softly in English as he sang in Portuguese.

The service ended. Keith put a hand under Dani's elbow to steer her around the clusters of people in the aisles. A few people greeted them as they edged their way to the door. He ignored their speculative glances and led Dani to the car.

"Now you're really going to get mixed up culturally," he warned. "I'm taking you downtown to a Chinese restaurant."

"I assumed we'd go back to the center. I don't have enough money. I was planning to fix something simple at my place."

"I distinctly remember telling you Friday that we'd see the zoo Sunday afternoon," he said with a sparkle in his eye. He wasn't letting Dani out of this one. "That means eating out, since it's too much driving to go all the way back to the center and then into downtown again."

"Oh. You didn't mention it yesterday."

"Thought I'd forgotten, huh? I don't forget things easily. Don't worry. I'll treat for lunch."

"Only if you let me fix you a meal in exchange."

"That is a deal."

The lunch crowd had not yet arrived, which suited Keith. They picked a table in a corner.

The restaurant decor was red and black. Eyes wide, Dani stared at the symbols and paintings. "I've never been to a Chinese restaurant before," she murmured. "Mom and Dad didn't take us out to eat often."

"Then I guess I should order."

"Unless you want me to talk to them in English."

"Want to try using chopsticks to eat?" he teased.

"Do you want to sit here the rest of the day while I try to move grains of cooked rice from the bowl to my mouth?"

He grinned. "Point conceded."

The delicious food was quite satisfying. Keith paid. Then they drove to the zoo. Although Dani had enough *cruzados* for the low entrance fee, he insisted on paying for both of them.

"Does this mean another meal at my place?" she asked.

"If you're offering, I'm taking."

"Maybe you should wait until you've tasted my cooking the first time. You might prefer your own."

"Why? Do you flavor it with paint or chalk?"

"Mmm. I should try that sometime."

She was fun to tease. He liked her quick wit.

Many families were at the zoo. They strolled leisurely on the sandy paths. Excited children exclaimed over this or that animal display. Well, not just the children . . .

Dani, too, was fascinated with the eel and the manatee ponds. She also had trouble moving past the various parrot cages.

Several times Keith laid a hand on hers to stop her from opening her sketchpad. "Just look at the displays today. You can return another day to draw. I want to see you just enjoy them today."

Her action was clearly reflexive, though. She started to open the pad again.

"Give me your right hand!" He pulled it through the crook of his left arm and turned them toward the monkey cages. "This is one way to keep your drawing hand occupied. You need to relax."

She tried to pull away. "But drawing is relaxing to me."

He tightened his grip. "Is it? Don't you realize you get keyed up? Like you've got to get it on paper quick—before it moves or changes?"

She halted and looked into his eyes. "I know I concentrate, but 'keyed up'?"

"Yes. I'm not saying it's wrong. In fact, it's probably one of the reasons you're such a good artist. But everyone needs a day off. You already drew in Sunday school. And I'm going to ask you to go to Júlio Cesar tomorrow with me to sketch my plane. That is, if you feel up to it."

She hesitated only a heartbeat. "Sure, Keith. I'd be happy to."

FOUR

"May I touch it?" Dani stood next to a Cessna 206 with registration letters KCT.

"Of course you may," Keith responded. "You've never flown in a small plane?"

She ran her hand along the fuselage. "No. I'd never been in a jet either. My trip here was very special. Nine hours of aerodynamic wonder."

"When I taxi KCT back to the Airclub hangar later, you can ride along. And sometime I'll take you up for a ride. You'll love it."

Dani wrinkled her nose. "I don't know. A jet's bigger and has extra engines in case something happens to one of them. Flying this baby must be dangerous."

"The most dangerous part of my day is the drive to and from the airport."

"Thinking of the traffic Friday by the bus station, that isn't saying a whole lot, Mr. Pilot."

"I promise you, the safety statistics are heavily in favor of flying versus driving when considering crashes."

"If you keep KCT in a different hangar, why did you bring it to this one?"

"The law requires a plane to be inspected in a licensed inspection station, which is what Bentes has. I have to get him to sign off each 50- or 100-hour inspection. I can't sign the paperwork because I'm not licensed in Brazil. I'm very thankful for a good working relationship with Bentes."

Keith turned as two men walked out of the nearby office. "Dani, let me introduce you to *Senhor* Bentes and one of his pilot/mechanics, Kiko. This is Daniela, an artist at the center."

The two Brazilians greeted her. She smiled and shook their hands.

The younger man held her hand longer than necessary and inquired in accented English, "Do you find Belém agreeable, *Senhorita* Daniela?"

She extracted her hand from his. "Yes, thank you."

The men began to speak in Portuguese with Keith, but Kiko flashed her an occasional smile. The older man walked away to check out the activity in the rest of his large hangar, which housed a helicopter and several planes.

"Kiko's going to help me with KCT," Keith explained. "The baffle has a few cracks, which he'll patch for me. I'm going to take the wheels off one at a time, clean and inspect them, grease the bearings, etcetera, which are all part of the 50-hour inspection."

Keith turned toward Kiko. "Say, do you have a chair or stool Daniela could sit on while she draws?"

"I'll get one." Kiko found a stool, dusted it off, and laid a clean towel over it to make sure Dani wouldn't get her culottes greasy. "If I may be of further service, don't hesitate to ask."

"Thanks, Kiko. She'll be fine," Keith replied before she could. He placed the stool where she wouldn't be in the way of any workers or planes. "If you need anything else, Dani, just holler."

"Thank you. I'll try to not disturb you." Dani took up her sketchpad and pencil but studied the Cessna for a full five minutes before laying down the proportions on paper. Before long she was engrossed in drawing and filled pages with sketches.

"Lunch break," Keith announced.

"Already?"

"Can I see what you've done?" He looked over her shoulder and whistled at a sketch of the whole plane.

She slowly turned back several pages so he could see three more, which were enlarged details of portions of KCT. She studied his face. "Do you like them?"

"They're great. You have real talent. I should frame them."

She shook her head. "I need to do more work on them. I'm just practicing. They're not good enough for framing."

"I think so. Hey, Kiko, what do you think of these pictures?"

Kiko joined them. "They're very good. Do you draw people also? Could you draw me with the helicopter?" he asked eagerly.

Dani glanced at Keith. He frowned, which she took as her cue. "I'll probably be very busy at the center once everyone returns from the conference."

"That's right," Keith agreed. "Now, if you'll excuse us for a while, we're going to eat lunch."

Kiko bowed slightly. "Of course."

Keith led her to a breezy spot by the side of the hangar. Dani's hair blew around her head. She tried to smooth it.

"Don't worry, Dani. I'm the only one here to see it. No candid camera."

"Which is why you've left the grease streak on your cheek?"

He swiped at his cheek but made the streak longer. Dani giggled. He pulled a handkerchief from his pocket and passed it to her. "Will you do the honors?"

"Why should I wipe it off when it's so becoming?" And then inspiration struck. Kiko had asked for a picture with himself and the helicopter. Instead, she would draw Keith. He looked so cute with that grease streak.

She could sketch him while he finished checking the wheels. Later, she could combine a couple of the sketches into a pastel of Keith standing next to KCT. She adored the medium of pastels. It would give her a good excuse to create more than the pencil sketches. Maybe she could give the finished product to him for his birthday—he'd said it was next month.

"Dani. Dani, are you there?" Keith chuckled as he waved one hand in front of her face.

Her brain still in gear, eyes wide with the new idea, she turned toward him. He was watching her carefully.

"What's going on behind those lively brown eyes?" he murmured.

"Oh, just an idea for a picture." She hoped he attributed her blush to the warmth of the day.

"Do you often get struck with ideas and look like you're a million miles away?"

"Yeah. I guess it's an occupational hazard with artists."

His eyes narrowed. "You need a bodyguard to protect you when you get lost in daydreams."

"Are you applying for the job, Mr. Pilot?" she asked sarcastically. "I am not a kid."

"Dani," he patiently explained, "you aren't safe in this culture unless you stay alert and take the necessary precautions to protect yourself and your belongings. You scare me sometimes."

Rather than answer him, she unwrapped the sandwich she'd brought.

"Would you like me to say grace?" Keith asked gently.

"Sure."

"Lord," he prayed, "thank You for a beautiful day and the food You've provided through the monetary gifts from people back home. Thank You for bringing Dani to Brazil. Bless her, Lord, and make her pictures a blessing to the translators and Indians. Guide me as I finish the inspection, that I might catch any discrepancies and fix them before they become a problem. In Jesus' Name, Amen."

His prayer mollified her. They began to munch their sandwiches. He'd brought a large thermos of water, which he shared after she declined his offer to buy her a soft drink.

She washed down a bite. "Tell me how you became interested in missionary aviation."

"My dad owns an F.B.O."

"A what?"

"Fixed-base operation—an airplane maintenance facility at an airport. I grew up around planes and learned to fly at an early age. I got my private pilot's license the day I turned 17 and my commercial pilot's license at 18. I racked up flight time before I went to college.

"I'd always thought I was a Christian; I went to church every Sunday with my family. But through a campus outreach group I discovered Christianity was more than attending church and being good. I began a personal relationship with Jesus Christ and started reading the Bible.

"My junior year, my roommate took me to hear a missionary speak about millions of people who don't have even one word of the Bible in their own language. He told about Bible translation for indigenous language groups around the world and the support team needed to do that work. I was amazed to learn I could use my pilot and mechanic skills in missionary aviation. I could fly men and women into remote locations so they could learn the language of some new group and translate God's Word into it. Bingo! I knew what I wanted to do with the rest of my life.

"Despite their own religious background, my parents didn't understand missions. They thought I'd joined some cult." He shrugged and skipped ahead. "I've been here a little over three years, but I didn't fly right away. I studied Portuguese the first eight months."

"How do your parents feel now?"

"They want me back home. My two younger brothers help Dad at the airport, but Dad always expected me to take over the business someday. I wish they'd visit me. I'd fly them to a few villages so they could see the importance of Bible translation. They've swallowed the line that Indians are happy in their old ways, so we shouldn't mess with their culture. If they could only see how many Indians are enslaved to fear, bound to spirit worship, before the missionary teaches them about God and His love.

"But, enough about me for now. How did you decide to trade in your life back home for a life in Belém?"

"My aunt and uncle taught missionary kids at a school in the Pacific for years, so I've always known about missions. I became a Christian when I was little; I can't pinpoint an exact time or date like some people can. But I know Jesus is my Savior.

"I grew up with a pencil in my hand, or a crayon, or piece of chalk. I was taking classes at a local art school when I heard there was a need for someone to illustrate books in Indian languages. Convincing my parents to let me travel here was difficult, since I'm the baby of the family and the only girl. But I reassured them that I'm just here for one year or less, so they finally gave in. The faster I draw, the sooner the job is completed, and I can go home."

"Not so, young lady. The faster you draw, the more work the translators discover needs to be done, and they keep you forever, if possible."

Dani laughed with him and downed the last of the water. "Sorry. I can't believe how thirsty I am."

"The heat and humidity take it out of you. I'll buy you bottled water later if you want more."

He stood. They walked back to the plane so Keith could work on the last wheel.

Dani took the opportunity to sketch him while she was supposed to be drawing KCT from other angles. She made quick sketches of several facial expressions and knew she'd captured him on paper. When Kiko sauntered over to talk, she flipped the pad face down before he saw she wasn't drawing the plane.

Later, when she was sketching the tail, the Brazilian brought her an ice cream bar. "For you, Daniela."

"Mmm. Thank you."

"When you see a street vendor, you can safely eat if it is this brand," he said. "At least that's what Kelcey told me."

"Hey, don't I get one, too?" Keith called.

"You're fluent enough to buy your own," Kiko answered. "I only help ladies in need."

Keith snorted. He edged closer and frowned until Kiko left.

Dani closed the sketchpad and slipped it and the pencils into her shoulder bag. She stood and stretched.

"Tired?" Keith asked. "Looks as though I'm not going to finish the inspection today after all. I'll take you home soon. You're not used to this sweltering heat. Girls tire out sooner."

"Hey, I'm fine. I just needed to change position. The stool won't win any design awards for comfort."

"I'll have to give you a rain check on taxiing back to the hangar in KCT. What are we doing for supper tonight?" His hazel eyes sparkled as he waited for a reaction.

Dani blinked. "I thought I'd make spaghetti."

"Yummy."

"I guess I do owe you one for yesterday."

"Two, actually. I paid for the zoo also."

"Ah, yes. Well, just remember I draw better than I cook."

"I'll take my chances."

On the way home, Dani prayed silently. *Lord, would it be too much to ask You for supper to be edible? You know my culinary skills lack finesse. I'm not asking it to be gourmet, but it would be so nice if the noodles don't glob together and the sauce is tasty. I know this is a trite request with all the other things going on in the universe, but I thank You for caring about all the details of our lives.*

A half hour after Keith dropped her off at her apartment, he returned. Dani was tossing the salad.

"Hmmm," he sniffed. "Dani's Italian restaurant."

"I hope the food tastes as good as the smell, but I'm still trying to get used to the iodine flavor on the lettuce and tomatoes."

He nodded. "That does take some adjustment, even if it is a necessary health precaution."

The conversation during the meal was light. Keith regaled her with tales about his flights and shared some of his funny goofs during language learning.

He thanked her for the good meal and left before Kristy arrived for the night. Maybe he'd known the child would jump to wrong conclusions if she saw him at Dani's.

Dani spent all day Tuesday working on the pastel and made good progress. Keith went to the airport again to finish the inspection on KCT after she assured him she'd be fine at the center.

Late in the afternoon, she heard footsteps on the sidewalk. She quickly laid the pastel on the closet shelf.

"Knock, knock," Maggie called out. "Hi, Dani. I thought you might be lonely. Would you care to join Ruth and me for aerobics and a dip in the school's pool?"

"Sounds great. I'll need a few minutes to change."

"Take your time." Her eyes rested on Dani's chalk-stained hands. "Been drawing?" She looked around the apartment, but only the pastel box was still on the table.

"Yes, I have." Dani didn't see the need to elaborate. She washed her hands at the kitchen sink.

"You'll want to wear some type of cover-up over your suit," Maggie suggested.

"Sure." Dani laid her beach towel on the table and went into the bathroom to pull on her swimsuit. She covered it with shorts and a tank top.

Ruth was waiting for them in an air-conditioned room with a TV and VCR. She turned on the video after she greeted Dani.

Maggie looked trim and toned. Her blonde hair was swept perfectly into a French braid with not one lock out of place. During a pulse break she asked, "Do you exercise regularly?"

Dani's curly top hadn't cooperated with her hairbrush in the extreme humidity, and she felt at a distinct disadvantage. "Not daily," she confessed, "but I try to get in aerobics or a long walk three days a week, which doesn't always work because I tend to get absorbed in drawing and forget everything else."

"You're welcome to join us anytime. We have the room reserved each weekday at this time."

"Thanks. I'll keep it in mind."

They took a short dip in the pool to cool off. Dani would have swum more than 10 laps, but her friends were toweling off. She thanked the two women and walked home. She anticipated leftover spaghetti and the prospect of another night with her talkative, nine-year-old chaperone. She was washing the supper dishes when the phone rang.

"Daniela, you have an outside call." Keith's voice sounded constrained, but she had no time to ask why or what he meant by an "outside call" before she heard a click.

"Hello, Daniela?" said an accented male voice.

"Yes?"

"This is Kiko Macedo. How are you this lovely evening?"

"Fine." Why would he be phoning her?

"Are you still working on the airplane pictures?"

"Yes. But the translators will be back soon. I'll begin drawing for them."

"I wonder if you might have a bit of time tonight to give me a little help over the phone with my English? I'm listening to a tape and have questions on the lesson."

"I . . . sure." She was too surprised to wonder why he hadn't asked Keith for help instead. For 25 minutes she tried to answer his multitude of questions. She gently corrected his pronunciation.

At last he said, "I'd love to talk with you in person. Would you have dinner with me tomorrow night? We could speak English, or I could teach you some Portuguese. I know a nice restaurant. Has Kelcey taken you out for *churrasco*?"

"*Shoe-HAWS-ku*? No. What is it?"

"A Brazilian specialty. You must try it."

The invitation stunned her. But Kiko was Keith's friend, and she had been properly introduced to him, so nothing should be wrong with accepting the invitation. "Sounds interesting."

"I'll pick you up at the gate at 7:30. Or, if you tell the guard to expect me, I can drive to your door. Which house are you in? Are you near Kelcey?"

She didn't like his inflection on the last question but squelched a retort. She didn't owe him an explanation, or the information of which apartment she was in. "I'll be at the gate. I don't know how to tell the guard anything yet."

"Then good night, Daniela. I'll see you in 24 hours."

FIVE

"Because we have only one outside phone line for the whole center, monopolizing it for close to 30 minutes isn't wise." Keith had practiced this sentence until he could say it without revealing his annoyance.

"I understand, Keith. I'm sorry. I won't let it happen again."

He had found Dani on the sidewalk by the Addisons' unpainted picket fence. She was sketching their blue macaw in its cage on the other side of the fence.

"Shall I tell Kiko if he phones again tonight?" Keith asked.

"That won't be necessary. He's taking me to a restaurant so he can practice English and teach me some Portuguese."

"He's what?" Keith exploded.

Dani flinched. She pulled the sketchpad against her chest and took a step back. "Why are you yelling at me?"

"Kiko is taking you out tonight?"

"Yes. I thought he was your friend. You introduced us."

Keith attempted to rein in his temper. "He's merely an acquaintance. A big difference. You can't go."

"What do you mean I can't go? Do you have something else planned? I don't remember you saying—"

"I said you can't go with him."

Dani squared her shoulders. "I'm 20 years old. Give me one good reason why I can't go out on a date."

"He's out of your league!"

"You're yelling again. And what do you mean?" Dani asked, insulted by his remark.

He raked a hand through his auburn hair. "I may trust Kiko to help fix my plane, but I wouldn't trust him one inch with you. He's not a Christian, and well . . ." How could he put it delicately enough for her? His face felt flushed; he hoped it wasn't apparent to her. Why couldn't she make this easier? "He thinks

differently. I don't like how he looks at some of the women passengers who fly in Bentes's aircraft."

Her eyes narrowed and she cocked her head. "Do you mean
he won't respect me—as a woman?"

He noted with some satisfaction the blush that spread in her
cheeks as soon as the words left her mouth. At least she was
understanding his implications now. "Yeah."

Her shoulders drooped. "He . . . seemed like a gentleman.
How can I back out now?"

"ARWAAAK! *ARARA! ARARA!*" the macaw squawked.

Dani jumped. "What does that mean?"

"'Parrot.' It just means 'parrot.'"

"I asked how I can back out at this point?"

His answer was low and gruff. "The only way you're leaving this center with Kiko Macedo tonight is if I go along."

"Wouldn't that look good," she scoffed.

"Listen, why don't I ask Maggie to go, and we'll double
date? You'll be safe and also save face. And when he asks you
out again, you can say no."

She exhaled in exasperation. "Are you sure he's like that? I
mean, this could look rather dumb."

"Trust me, Dani. I'm responsible for you, at least until
tomorrow morning when the first of the Belém bunch returns
from the conference. Your safety is my concern. I don't think
you're safe with Kiko."

"So who's going to tell Kiko? You expect me to?"

"I'll phone him and take care of it."

"I'm sorry I'm such a bother," she huffed. Clutching her
sketchpad and pencils, she walked away.

Keith fell into step beside her. He was amused when she
stiffened her back. "You're not going to finish the drawing?"

"I don't feel like drawing anymore."

"So, did he mention a particular restaurant?"

"Something about a shoe."

He smothered a laugh. "*Churrascaria?*"

"Not exactly. Something like that. I don't know. Could I be
alone for a while, please?"

"Sure, Dani."

He watched her retreat to her apartment. Younger brothers he knew how to manage, but he'd never had a sister. She was like a volcano ready to erupt with hot tears of embarrassment. A cute volcano, at that. He shook his head. She was too trusting for her own good.

Protect her, Lord! Keep her out of trouble when she jumps into situations she knows nothing about. Forgive me for losing my cool with her. And please give me wisdom to deal with her until the others return tomorrow.

Maggie and Keith arrived at Dani's apartment at 7:20. Maggie looked stunning, her apricot linen dress perfect for her figure and blonde coloring.

Dani wore a blue, cotton chambray dress printed with tiny, white flowers. Her hair fairly cooperated, which was a relief. Yet she felt so nervous about this double date, she wished she'd never traveled to Belém. Her stomach churned.

"Stop pacing and relax," Keith said. "Everything will work out. Kiko will probably be late. I told the guard to direct him here."

"Maybe he won't show." She could always hope. "Maggie, I appreciate your willingness to help out. I've never been in such a muddle before. It's humiliating."

"Keith's right. Relax. I'm glad Kiko asked you out because then Keith asked me out. So, you see, I have you to thank for this occasion. And I do enjoy eating out."

"I gave Rebecca and John the extra key to your apartment so Kristy can get in," Keith said. "They agreed she'll be all right for a while with the door locked and a book to read should we get back a little late."

"Thanks."

Kiko pulled his car up in front of Dani's promptly at 7:30. One point in his favor. And he acted like the double date had been part of his original plan. Another point in his favor. He complimented hers and Maggie's dresses, then cupped Dani's elbow and led her out to the car. He seated her in the front seat, while Keith assisted Maggie into the back.

Kiko drove several miles to the restaurant. The air in the parking lot was laden with the delicious smell of roasting meat.

Kiko led Dani to a table for four. The men sat on either side of her, with Maggie across the table. A waiter appeared. The men ordered soft drinks.

The Brazilian pilot turned to Keith. "I'll ask you to explain the meal to Daniela. You know all the English words."

"Sure." Keith's hazel eyes met her brown ones. "Different waiters bring cuts of meat, each on a skewer, to the table. Use your fork to point to the part of the meat you'd like to have. The waiter slices off that piece, and it drops onto your plate. They keep returning and offering you meat until you say, *'Obrigada.'*"

"Say that again, slowly, please!"

"Females say *'o-bri-GA-da.'* It means 'thank you.' But in this context it denotes 'enough, no more, thank you.' Fried bananas, rice, beans, and some other foods will be brought out and served family style at the table. But the main attraction here is the meat."

"Roast beef, chicken, tongue, liver, and several kinds of sausage are some of the cuts included," Maggie added. "All are roasted over an open flame. They taste delicious. I love *churrasco.*"

"That's the word," Dani said to Keith. "The word Maggie just used." Maggie looked puzzled, but Keith nodded. He turned to Kiko.

"Thanks for repairing the baffle for KCT. You did a great job, as always."

"You're welcome. I believe Bentes signed the papers this afternoon, so your plane is ready to fly once more."

The waiters began bringing meat. Dani imitated her friends. She held up her fork, poked into the roast where it looked well done, and poked the lowest piece of chicken and sausage on the other skewers. She also tried each of the side dishes brought to their table. She liked the bananas, rice, and potato salad more than the meat, but her companions made up for her indifference. If she had to choose one of the meats, though, she would pick the barbecued chicken as her favorite. She couldn't get excited about tongue, liver, or heart, and the sausages tasted too spicy.

Kiko ordered another round of soft drinks. "This meal always makes me so thirsty."

"Because the chefs use lots of salt on the meat," Maggie responded. "I'll be thirsty all night, but it's worth eating here occasionally. Reminds me of barbecues back home."

Dani ate more potato salad while the others chewed on roast. The soft drink Kiko had ordered for her was *Guaraná*. She had never tasted anything like it and found it difficult to finish.

Kiko leaned close, as he did each time he spoke to her. "It is a distinctly Brazilian flavor, Daniela." She wanted to back away from him but didn't want to appear rude.

"You'll like it more after you've lived here longer," he added. "You should try many new flavors and foods. We have a rich variety in Brazil."

When everyone was full, Kiko split the bill with Keith and then led the way to the car. "Shall we drive downtown for some ice cream?" Kiko asked.

Maggie groaned. "I should walk a couple of miles first. I'm stuffed."

"You can diet tomorrow," Kiko laughed. "All women say that after eating out. Yet I can see no reason for you to diet." His appraising look at Maggie's figure made Dani blush.

"Kiko," Keith warned.

"Ice cream would taste good, I think," the Brazilian said.

"You're the driver," Keith conceded.

They drove to a Cairú ice cream shop, where Dani studied the list mounted on the wall. Such a multitude of flavors from which to choose! She couldn't decipher even half the names.

"Don't feel embarrassed," Keith said. "Most of these flavors are Brazilian fruits not grown in the States."

"Try this purple one called *açaí*." Kiko put one arm around her shoulders and tapped the glass display with his other hand.

"*Ah-sigh-EE*." Dani sidestepped out of his reach. "I'd rather have plain old vanilla, please. I've had enough new experiences tonight."

"You should be more adventuresome!" Kiko chided. "Next time, perhaps."

He didn't know a next time was not going to occur, but she couldn't exactly announce that in front of the others. She was too kind-hearted to embarrass him.

"Here, taste the *bacurí*." Maggie held a tiny wooden spoon out to Keith, who sampled some.

"Ah, yes," Kiko said. "Would you like a taste of mine? I should have thought of that."

Dani shook her head. "No, thank you. The vanilla tastes great."

During the walk back to the car, Kiko put an arm around her waist. She tensed. His arm tightened. He murmured close to her ear, "On weekends we have many more things to do and see. We could go out again. Maybe you'd like Mosqueiro Beach, which isn't far away. My family has a beach house. We could spend the day there. Or the whole weekend."

The inference of his words and his touch scared her. "No. Thank you." *Keith! Don't walk so far ahead!* her mind screamed. She managed to step out of his hold.

In the car on the way home, the two pilots conversed, allowing Dani much-needed relief and space. She pondered what this date would have been like without Keith and Maggie along. *Bless you, Keith, for insisting on the double date.*

Kiko pulled off BR-316 and approached the gate. "Which house is yours, Maggie?"

"You can drop us off at Daniela's," Keith replied. "We'll walk from there. The evening is so nice."

Kiko opened his mouth as if to argue but closed it. He pulled up in front of Dani's apartment and opened the passenger door for her. Keith and Maggie got out on the passenger side also and stood with them.

"Thanks for taking us, Kiko," Keith said.

"Yes, thank you," Dani echoed. "The meal was delicious. I hope we were able to help you with your English."

"Very much. Good night." He drove away.

Dani sagged against the doorpost and exhaled. "I thought the evening would never end."

"He took it rather well," Maggie observed aloud.

Keith grinned. "I believe he got the hint. He didn't say, 'See you soon.'"

Good thing he didn't know what Kiko had suggested outside the ice cream store. She could picture the anger that would swell up inside Keith. Who needed big brothers for protection when Keith Kelcey was around to serve in their place?

"I ate too much. My head is pounding," Dani admitted. "I'm calling it a day. Thank you both for going. Good night."

Surprisingly, Kristy was already asleep in her hammock. This was her last night to stay with Dani. Keith would be picking up several *Kombi*-loads of fellow missionaries at the airport in the morning. Others would return at the end of the week after post-conference meetings.

Dani hung up her dress, pulled on a long T-shirt nightgown, and brushed her teeth. She slipped wearily into the bed.

Thank You, God, for working things out this evening. I am too tired to talk with You more, but I am grateful.

Tomorrow she'd swallow her pride and tell Keith he'd been right about Kiko.

At 3 a.m. Dani awoke terribly nauseated. She barely made it to the bathroom in time. Fortunately, Kristy slept through the noise. Dani eased back into bed, but, as soon as she was prone, the whole process repeated itself. Several times, in fact. Had she ever been so sick before?

By 5 a.m. she stopped counting the number of trips to the bathroom. She was so weak she slumped to the floor and laid her face on the cool linoleum. Moving to and from her bed was just too much work. Easier to stay right here and sleep . . ..

Keith pulled the loaded *Kombi* through the open gate and waved his thanks to the watchman. "Who wants to be dropped off first?"

"We're closest to the door, rather than have people climb over us," Eric Raymer said.

"Isn't that Kristy Holman?" his wife Jeni asked.

"What's she—?" Keith hit the brake pedal.

Kristy, in her nightgown, ran up to the vehicle. "Kelcey, help! Quick! She's lying on the bathroom floor and won't wake up!"

He didn't need to ask to whom she was referring. Had Dani fallen and hit her head? Keith put the *Kombi* in park and jumped out. "Eric, you take it." He ran to the apartment, with Kristy trailing behind.

A very pale Dani was curled up on the bathroom floor. He dropped to his knees beside her. He checked her pulse and looked for blood or bumps. She felt very cool to his touch. He ran his hand lightly over her head and neck; no bumps there either. What had happened to her?

"Is she diabetic?"

Jeni's voice surprised him. He hadn't heard her walk in but should have figured she'd follow. She was a nurse.

"Not that I know of. She never said. She doesn't wear one of those bracelets."

"Medic alert. She has no obvious broken bones. Apparently she didn't fall but just lay down there."

"What's wrong with her?" Kristy demanded.

"We don't know yet," Jeni answered.

Keith slid one arm under Dani's knees, the other under her shoulders, and scooped her off the floor. He carried her to the bed and laid her gently on it. "I'll phone the doc."

"Good idea." Jeni began timing Dani's pulse and respiration. "When did you last see her? Was she depressed? Could she have overdosed?" The questions were directed to him, not the child.

"No!" he emphasized. Dani had been relieved the evening was over. Yes, she'd had a headache, but Keith felt sure she would not have taken more than the proper dosage of aspirin. "Kristy, go ahead and get dressed and go home for some breakfast. I'm sorry this has scared you." Without looking up the number, he dialed the doctor's house.

Kristy shifted from one foot to the other and back again. "Is Dani going to the hospital?"

"This is Kelcey," he said into the phone in Portuguese. "We have an emergency. I need to speak to Doctor Farias."

Jeni smoothed Dani's nightgown and tucked the sheet around her. "Kristy, honey, do what Kelcey asked you. We'll let you know what the doctor says after he's checked Dani and made a diagnosis."

Dani opened her eyes later; she had no idea how much later. Although she was in her own room, a stranger sat next to her bed watching an I.V. drip into her arm. "Who—?"

The woman smiled reassuringly. "Hello, Dani. You're going to be all right."

"What happened?" Even whispering was an effort.

"You've been very ill—food poisoning, and then you became dehydrated, according to what Doctor Farias deduces. I'm Jeni Raymer. My husband and I do literacy work, but I'm also a nurse."

"Kristy?"

"She found you on the bathroom floor this morning around 6:30 and ran out of the apartment as we drove into the center. She yelled for Kelcey. He jumped out of the *Kombi* before I even blinked. He phoned the doctor."

"How long ago?" Dani forced her eyes to stay open.

"Five and a half hours. It's noon now."

Dani focused on the I.V. "I'm in my own bed."

"Yes. We talked the doctor into letting you stay here rather than going to the hospital. We promised him we'd take good care of you. You're past the crisis but must rest and drink liquids until you can eat regular foods once more."

"Food poisoning. No one else got sick?"

"No. Keith and the doctor went over what you had eaten differently from the others last night, and they figured it had to be either the potato salad, or the vanilla ice cream, or both."

Keith knocked on the door and entered. He set a grocery bag on the counter. "Should I make up the gelatin?"

"In a while," Jeni replied. "You got some crackers, too?"

"Yes." He walked over to the side of the bed. "Hi, Dani. How do you feel?"

"Like a truck hit me." She tried to smile to let him know it was a joke, but a tear slipped down her cheek. "I'm sorry to be such a bother."

His eyes narrowed. "I'm the one who feels badly for you." He smiled gently. "Besides, you've already apologized at least once in the past."

"How long do I get this I.V.?"

"Doctor Farias will return to check on you around four this afternoon."

"If you're doing well," Jeni added, "we'll pull out the I.V. and start you on gelatin and crackers. Keith picked them up at the store."

"Thanks, but the thought of food makes me a little green still."

Jeni patted her hand. "That's to be expected. Give yourself another few hours. In fact, why don't you rest again?"

"OK." Dani sighed and closed her eyes. "Thank you."

S I X

Keith shut off the alarm clock, stretched, pulled on jeans and a shirt, and padded barefoot to his kitchen. He had enough time to fry an egg and make toast and coffee. His sack lunch and overnight bag were ready to go.

How was Dani feeling this morning? he wondered. He wished he could check on her, but he'd have to trust Jeni and the others to take care of her now. He needed to focus on his upcoming flight instead.

How much more baggage would Ned and Patti Phillips have this morning? Yesterday he'd weighed boxes and bags of supplies, but translators always found last minute items they wanted to take along. They were close to maximum weight already, so he hoped they didn't find too much, or they'd have to spend time figuring out what to leave behind for another flight and maybe repack a few boxes.

Would the Airclub workers have KCT parked at the front of the hangar as he'd requested? Or would it be blocked by several other aircraft?

He set his plate on the table, poured coffee and added milk, and sat down. *Lord, thank You for a new day and the opportunity to use my skills to serve You. I pray for a safe flight. I know today holds snags and surprises. Help me be patient and pleasant, even when things don't go as planned. Bless the Phillipses during this village stay. Bring more Poneraja into Your kingdom as they learn from Your Word who You are and how Your Son died for our sins. In Jesus' Name, Amen.*

After he ate, he washed the dishes, brushed his teeth, and pulled on socks and boots. He slipped his New Testament and Psalms into his shirt pocket. He'd get a chance to read later in the day or early evening.

At the old hangar, he unlocked the office. He reviewed his carefully prepared flight plan, slipped the papers onto his kneeboard, and phoned S.E.R.A.C. for a weather briefing. As he expected, the morning would be clear. They'd be safe on the ground at Poneraja before any afternoon storms threatened their flight.

Ned showed up as Keith unlocked the storage room next to the office. The two men loaded the boxes into the *Kombi*.

Patti scurried into view with two nylon sacks. "Sorry! I've got a bit more to go with us."

Keith set the items on the freight scale and mentally added them to yesterday's total. He exhaled in relief. "You're right at the limit, Patti, unless either of you gained weight this morning."

She laughed. "All I ate was a muffin, so don't look at me. Who's driving us?"

"Eric. He'll be here any minute." Keith tossed his gear into the *Kombi*.

Eric Raymer walked around the corner of the building. "Hi everyone. I'm not late, am I?"

"Just on time." Ned motioned his wife into the middle seat.

Keith padlocked the storage and office doors, and then handed Eric the car keys. "Did Jeni stay with Dani last night?" he asked softly.

"Yes. They did fine. I've already been by there to check."

"Thanks."

Eric cocked his head. "Do I detect some personal interest in that kid?"

"Hey, I was supposed to be watching out for her while you all were in Brasilia, not letting her almost die from food poisoning. Let's get going." Keith slipped into the passenger seat and snapped the seat belt.

Let it go, buddy. Keith tried to stop picturing Dani on the floor or lying in her bed with an I.V. in her arm. *You have a job to do today.*

At the airport he filed his flight plan while workers moved several planes to get KCT out. He did his walk around, checked for water in the fuel, and loaded the baggage and passengers into the plane. He made sure the center of gravity was at the rear limit by pushing the tail down until it almost touched the ground and then releasing it, allowing it to return to its original position, just as it should.

"You forgot to warn your passengers you were going to do that," Eric pointed out with a grin.

"Ned and Patti are quite used to the procedure after all the years they've been flying. I only have to remind you new guys," Keith countered.

"Should I pick you up tomorrow? You can radio Tammy your E.T.A. She can let me know."

"Thanks, Eric, but I'll just catch a cab back to the center."

"OK. Have a good flight."

Keith waited until Eric backed away from the plane before he climbed in. He ran through the checklist. Soon they were airborne.

The precise moment of lift off never ceased to thrill and amaze him. *Thank You, God, for letting man figure out Your principles of aerodynamics. I love seeing Your world from up here. People might look like dots, but You know each of us by name and love us more than we can ever fathom. Thank You.*

He radioed to his flight-follower, Tammy, his flight information, as he climbed to 5,500 feet in the air. He told her his lift-off time; estimated time en route: two hours; destination: Poneraja; E.T.A. of the next checkpoint; weight on takeoff; amount of fuel in the tanks; and the number of people on board: three. He listened as she repeated the information.

While he'd been trained to navigate by dead reckoning— using compass heading and time between checkpoints, Keith hoped the mission would soon install G.P.S. in each of its planes. He was very interested in the safety that technology promised.

Two hours later he set KCT down on the grass strip at Poneraja. The plane rolled to a stop. He cut the engine, got out, and assisted the Phillipses.

Most of the villagers had arrived to greet them. He recognized Ebano, the main translation helper, and Siri, the chief of the village. He hoped to learn a few more names on this visit.

Within a minute those who were tall enough pressed noses against KCT's Plexiglas windows to peer inside. Kids ran around laughing and asking what was in the boxes Keith was unloading from the pod.

Keith didn't have to know the language to guess what they were saying. Kids were kids. He smiled and greeted them with the two words Patti had taught him on the last flight. They laughed at his pronunciation and chattered away.

He'd have the rest of the day to learn new words. He had no illusions about having peace and quiet to help Ned and Patti get set up. The kids would hound his every step and ask questions. Maybe he should be glad he didn't speak their language.

Various village men carried the boxes up the path to the Phillipses' adobe-with-aluminum-roof house. A supply of kerosene had been trucked in, so Keith volunteered to check over the stove and fridge and get tanks hooked to them while Ned and Patti cleaned, unpacked, and organized the house.

At lunchtime, Keith walked down to the river with his sack lunch. A dozen kids followed him. He didn't have enough food to share, so he smiled and ate, trying not to let their stares bother him.

The first time he'd flown into a village, he'd carried a sack of candies. The translators had quickly confiscated them, explaining to Keith that he shouldn't set a precedent. Not only would the children expect him to bring them something every time, but the candy wasn't good for their teeth, either.

A few kids jumped in the cold water and started splashing each other. Siri's son, Bufo, headed toward Keith, but he jumped up and moved away from the shore. He would swim with them later.

What would Dani think if she could see these kids, this village? What would she choose to draw?

He thought again of the sketches he'd seen in her sketchpad the first morning, of the way she'd drawn KCT at Bentes's. He was absolutely amazed at her incredible talent. Yet she admitted her mechanical skills were limited to changing a light bulb. Keith grinned. God sure had a sense of humor when He gifted people in various ways.

His next project was to clean the rain barrel. He poured out the stagnant water and scrubbed the inside of the barrel. With the way the clouds were building, they'd get some fresh water by late afternoon.

"Would you check on the boat engine for me?" Ned asked. "Here's the key to the shed."

"Should I get some men to help me pull the boat to the shore?"

"No, I'll ask them to do that later."

Keith made sure the engine ran properly. Then he took time to hang his hammock with its mosquito netting under the thatch-roof shelter next to the house.

Children kept tagging him. Several times he'd turn quickly and laughingly tag them back. With no more chores to do, he had time to cool off in the river before the storm. He borrowed the bedroom for a few minutes of privacy to change into his swim trunks and put flip-flops on his feet.

At the river's edge he laid down his towel and took off the flip-flops. Immediately a girl about seven years old put on the huge footwear. Everyone laughed as she tried to walk in them and as she shuffled around the shore.

For the next half hour boisterous children splashed and tagged Keith as they played. Bufo, in particular, seemed to delight in out-maneuvering Keith, as if it were a test of his skill and cunning. As son of the chief, he probably felt the need to prove himself.

The sky darkened; the wind picked up. Just before the storm hit, the children dashed off to their respective homes. Keith wrapped the towel around his shoulders and went back to the house.

So many women visitors had interrupted Patti's unpacking, she hadn't even started supper preparations. Keith pitched in and cooked the rice, while Patti heated canned stew to put over it. They ate canned fruit and packaged cookies for dessert.

Rain pounded the aluminum roof and made conversation impossible. Keith volunteered to wash the dishes. Then the three adults sat in the living room and read a while.

Keith pulled the New Testament from his pocket. One day the Poneraja people would have this book in their language. They already had quite a bit of it in machine-copied booklets.

The church was growing. A training retreat for leaders was planned for the fall. Keith would be called on to fly men into this central location from various villages. He felt privileged that God allowed him to have a small part in getting the Bible to these people.

"I'm exhausted. I didn't get much sleep last night." Patti stood and kissed her husband. "Good night."

"Don't worry about fixing me a breakfast," Keith said. "I can grab a bread roll and some jelly before I leave."

"You know where I keep the instant coffee, too." Patti yawned.

Ned stood. "Are you heading out at dawn?"

"Probably. I usually wake early when I'm sleeping outside."

Keith wanted to get back to Belém as soon as possible so he could beat the afternoon rain—and to make sure Dani was better. After all, he'd been responsible to protect her and had failed. If only he'd told her to avoid eating the potato salad or the ice cream . . .

"Thanks for bringing us and for all your help setting up. See you again in two months. If all goes as we hope and pray, we'll be able to celebrate the completed rough draft of the New Testament."

"Wonderful!"

"You've got your flashlight handy for finding your hammock? Will you extinguish the lantern when you finish reading?"

"Sure. Good night."

The Indian agent for the Poneraja roused Keith before dawn. "We have a medical emergency. I need you to fly two people out. Pantera is writhing in pain. From what he describes, and from my own experience, I'd guess he has a kidney stone. The nearest town is Brinco. Ebano will go along."

"All right. Give me 15 minutes. I'll see you at the plane."

Keith had slept in his clothes. He made sure no critters had crawled into his boots, put them on, and rolled up his hammock. He tiptoed into the kitchen, took a roll and a few cookies, and refilled his drinking cooler with room-temperature water from the water filter. He'd forego the jelly and coffee. He had planned to refuel at Brinco anyway, so this trip wouldn't take him off course. No need to jot Ned and Patti a note; they'd hear about his passengers by breakfast time. The grapevine in villages worked as well or better than at the Belém center.

Keith walked to the airstrip and tossed his gear into the plane. The sky had lightened enough so he could do the walk-around and check the fuel.

The agent strode into view, followed by two men and two women. *I guess the wives are going along also.*

Keith took the change in stride and showed each one where to sit. He made sure their seat belts and harnesses were in place. Then he climbed in and went through his checklist. At least the agent would make sure no kids ran toward the plane should they show up at this early hour.

Twenty minutes later he landed at Brinco. Ebano thanked him and left to arrange transportation into the town. Keith checked his watch. Too early for buying fuel here.

He pulled out the bread and cookies, thankful his mom couldn't see his makeshift meal and lecture him on what a well-balanced breakfast should include. Some days he missed home. At least a little. But God had given him a task to fulfill; he willingly sacrificed to do it. He just wished his parents and brothers could visit Poneraja or another Indian village and get a tiny glimpse of the life-and-death necessity of giving God's Word to all people groups around the world.

What would his mom think of Dani? No, he wouldn't ponder that thought.

She'd always joked about being the only female in the family and being out-voted all the time. Some day she'd have a few daughters-in-law to even out the sides.

Whoa. How had his train of thought moved from breakfast, to Dani, to daughters-in-law? Was he so tired his mind was wandering? He should have prepared a cup of coffee before leaving Poneraja.

He checked his chronograph again. Tammy should have the radio turned on by now. He could crank the engine and radio in. Or he could see if any airport workers could tell him how soon

he could refuel the plane and get on his way. Maybe he'd even
ask where to buy some coffee . . ..

SEVEN

"We call this little booklet a *dolly*," Jeni said to Dani in the Literature Production office. "We make it from scrap paper and number the pages so we know which ones to paste up together and then which to copy back-to-back. Roy hopes you'll learn to do the paste-up as well as the drawings to save time for the translators and us literacy workers. Then all we'd have to do is copy off the number of booklets we need for the villages."

"How fascinating. I've never thought about how books are produced."

"You'd be especially good at it because you have an eye for balance. Part of laying out a booklet is figuring out where to put each picture, what size to make it, and how much copy would look good on each page." Jeni pointed at spaces on some of the computer printout pages. "We've all been cutting pictures out of old primers from other countries in which our mission works, reducing or enlarging them to fit the spaces. Now we'll have your drawings to use. But no need to start today if you're not up to it yet. We can wait, as long as we have the books before we go to the village in September."

"I've rested for days!" Dani lamented.

"We don't want you to overdo it, though, on your first day out."

"Everyone's been so helpful—and protective. But I'm fine now."

Jeni pulled out some photos and spread them on a long table. "OK, let me show you what we'd like. Here's a photo of a *tapir*. We'll also need a picture of a monkey, but I have no photo. You could make one up or else draw the small variety you see in the Belém zoo. The folk tale speaks of a panther-like cat, which you can find in the zoo also. Then we need some Indian men; I have various shots that might work. And we need you to draw an *açaí* tree; the center has several to use as models. Don't worry about getting the sizes perfect; you can reduce or enlarge when you use the copier."

"This gives me a good place to begin. Thanks, Jeni."

Dani set to work. After penciling several sketches, she went back over them with a fine, black-felt pen so the lines would show up when copied. She was still drawing at noon when Roy locked up his office nearby.

"Lunch time!" he called. "Here, I'll use my key to lock up the office until we can have one made for you."

She didn't look up from the page. "I'm almost finished. I'll just stay here."

"No you don't, Daniela. You've been sick. We can't let you skip lunch. The drawings have been on hold for a long time, so a few hours or days won't make much difference. Out you go. You've got to take care of yourself, you know. And be sure to take a *siesta* after lunch before you return. Tonight's prayer meeting night."

"Yes, sir." Dani laid down the pencil and closed the door to her office. Actually, she was tired. And she did manage to take a short nap.

When she walked into the meeting room that night, she was surprised to see Keith instead of Roy standing up front. He was talking with Maggie, who was seated in the first row of chairs next to Ruth. Did the school staff and mission meet together for the Wednesday night prayer times? Yet Maggie and Ruth were the only ones present from A.I.S. Were they attending the meeting because of Keith?

"You all know I greatly prefer flying to leading meetings," Keith began, "but my turn has once again rolled around. Let's begin with the hymn 'Jesus Loves Even Me.' This song has a message for all of us, no matter our age or people group. So think about the words as we sing."

> *I am so glad that our Father in Heav'n*
> *Tells of His love in the Book He has giv'n;*
> *Wonderful things in the Bible I see,*
> *This is the dearest, that Jesus loves me.*

I am so glad that Jesus loves me . . .
Jesus loves even me.

Oh, if there's only one song I can sing,
When in His beauty I see the great King,
This shall my song through eternity be,
"Oh, what a wonder that Jesus loves me!"

I am so glad that Jesus loves me . . .
Jesus loves even me.

"Each of us is precious in God's sight," Keith continued. "We may think we're not very lovable, but that's a lie from Satan. God, the Master Creator, formed us so we might honor and glorify Him. You've heard the saying, 'God doesn't make any junk.' Well, you can stop fretting about your hair being curly or straight, how tall or short you are, the freckles on your face, or the shape of your nose. God designed you and loves you.

"He thinks about you all the time. Psalm 40:5 says: 'Many, O Lord my God, are the wonders which You have done, and Your thoughts toward us; there is none to compare with You. If I would declare and speak of them, they would be too numerous to count.' Psalm 139:17-18a says: 'How precious also are Your thoughts to me, O God! How vast is the sum of them! If I should count them, they would outnumber the sand.'

"Can you count the grains of sand on the beach? No. Our finite minds can't count the sand on even one beach, let alone all the beaches in the world. But that's how much God thinks about each of us.

"He also loves the Indians with whom we work and those we haven't yet reached. Last week I had the privilege of taking Ned and Patti out to Poneraja. They hope to complete the rough draft of the New Testament this village visit, if they have the proper translation help and don't get interrupted too often.

"You and I can be part of that great work of God through our prayers. So tonight I want us to spend about 15 minutes praying for the list of Poneraja people I've written on the board, and for the Phillipses. Then we'll sing another song and take your prayer requests."

The hour passed quickly. Dani listened carefully, as she tried to learn more about the mission and its work. She wrote down names so she could keep praying for people during her own quiet times.

Keith may not have liked leading the meeting, but he spoke well in front of the group. Dani hoped only the men shared the task, for she'd hate to have to take a turn up front.

The following days fell into a routine. Work commenced with a half-hour prayer meeting each weekday morning, at the end of which Roy gave announcements. Eight translators attended: the Smiths and Martins, both with grown children in the States; the Addisons with two high school kids; and the Williamses with two young boys. The Tatums and Phillipses were flown to their villages while Dani was sick. Then there were "support" couples who helped out in various capacities. Keith attended when he wasn't on an early-morning flight.

Dani was too awed by the veteran missionaries to pray out loud as they did. She felt like a spiritual baby in their midst.

At 8:30 every weekday morning she'd walk past Gilda Dias's small cubicle and Roy's office and into the Literature Production office. Here she worked until lunchtime and again in the afternoon.

She was invited out for several suppers that week. Roy and Irene Davis asked her over; she met their children. Their 11-year-old son, Tommy, of whom Kristy had spoken, liked R.C. planes; his sister, Mary, was in junior high.

Conan Emery was the computer and radio specialist. His wife, Tammy, had a short-wave radio in their home office, so she could flight-follow Keith while she cared for two elementary school girls and a toddler.

"Tammy is a second-cousin to Brenda Tatum," Conan said. "Brenda and Ben are translators. I guess you haven't meet them yet."

"No, I haven't."

"They're a great couple. They should be back in September or October from a break."

Dani felt privileged to be associated with such fine, Christian people. It helped relieve the homesickness she was fighting. She had never been away from home for more than a week at a time. Irene had suggested she phone her parents occasionally, but when Dani heard the cost per minute, she balked. Writing letters would have to suffice.

As energy allowed, she worked nights on the pastel of KCT. She had drawn Keith standing next to the Cessna, one hand resting on the fuselage. His face was grease-streaked, but his expression showed the pride he had in his plane. She needed to chalk in the wings, the tail, and the propeller.

She waited a week after her recovery before she rejoined Maggie and Ruth for aerobics. She'd leave the office early but would work for an hour after supper most evenings to make up for the break.

In order to complete the sketches for Jeni and Eric Raymer, she needed to get to the zoo but was reluctant to ride the bus alone. She was afraid she'd miss the stop, and she still spoke only a few words of Portuguese.

Ruth offered to ride downtown with her one workday on her way to attend a meeting. They waited until the rush hour ended. Ruth showed Dani how to hail a bus. They climbed aboard via a door near the rear of the bus and paid the guy seated there to collect fares. Ruth motioned to an empty bench seat, then briefed her on which bus was best for returning to the center.

Dani blinked. "You mean I'm riding back alone?"

"No, dear. I'm just telling you for future reference. I'll meet you at the zoo. We'll ride home together. You did bring a sandwich, didn't you? Will 3 o'clock give you enough time for all you have to draw?"

"Oh, yes. I'll be done by then."

Dani sketched not only the monkeys but also an emu, a vulture, several of the colorful parrots, and the foliage growing along the shaded paths. People stood around her to watch and comment in Portuguese. All she could do was smile, nod, and hope they weren't asking questions.

Ruth was waiting at the gate when Dani exited the zoo. They walked around the huge block to a one-way street going out of town and caught a yellow bus. They sat two-thirds of the way forward in the only vacant bench seat.

Just before the bus reached the main highway out of town, the driver drove around a wicked curve at an alarming rate. Dani gasped and grabbed hold of the seat.

"They all drive like that," Ruth fussed. "Scares you half to death."

"Do these buses ever tip over?"

"Occasionally, but not as often as you'd think, considering how they drive."

More and more people piled on the bus until the aisle was full. Another person could not have squeezed in. Dani felt a rising panic and forced her claustrophobia into submission. "Don't they have a law about how many people can ride at one time?"

"Probably. But no one ever enforces it. The drivers take as many people as they can. Their bosses tell them to do it because it brings in more money for the company."

The two women had to push and shove to get off the bus. If they hadn't been seated near the front, Dani's sketchpad would probably have gotten bent and ruined, but they finally made it out into the fresh air at their stop.

Dani shivered as they walked down the entrance road to the center. "I don't want to try that again."

Ruth laughed. "You may not want to, but you will. The bus is the cheapest way to get to town. Mission vehicles aren't always available. You'll get used to it."

Another Sunday rolled around. The Addisons invited Dani to attend First Baptist with them and then go out to eat. The large church was just one block from the main plaza downtown. They had signed out the *Gol.* As she squeezed into the back seat with their two teenagers, Debbie and Paul, Dani forced her thoughts away from the confined space where she sat.

How is Keith getting to his church? she wondered. *What lesson is he teaching the kids today?*

"After the service we'll walk to the plaza and show you the Hippie Fair," Louise Addison said from the front seat.

"What is it?"

"Booths set up along the wide sidewalk with various crafts and foods people can buy. Vendors sell paintings, T-shirts, jewelry, wood decorations, trinkets, and more. I think you'll like it."

Dani did. The Addisons could hardly coax her away to go to the restaurant. Several of the paintings were gorgeous; she admired the work behind them. She could paint as well, or better, if she took the time. However, she wasn't in Belém to make money selling art but to illustrate books for nationals.

They ate at the *Avenida Restaurante*, which occupied the second floor of a corner building overlooking the *Praça Nazaré*. Jim and Louise Addison kept the conversation going. Dani learned about their work and village. She discovered both Paul and Debbie had positive outlooks about Bible translation; they felt needed and involved in what their parents were doing.

Back at her apartment, Dani decided to nap before writing her parents. She seemed to need more rest since she'd been sick. When she awoke, she began another letter home.

"Knock, knock!" Keith called from the porch by the kitchen window.

"Hey there!"

"Aha, writing a boyfriend back home?" He sat down next to her at the dining room table.

"Yeah. He's called 'Mom and Dad.'"

"And what's his last name?" Keith teased, the lights in his eyes dancing merrily. "Do you think I know him?"

"Only if you've been through Little City, U.S.A."

"I don't believe I have. What's it near?"

"A slightly bigger city."

He put his elbows on the table and leaned closer, his hazel eyes growing serious. "Have you told your family how ill you were from the food poisoning, how close you were to being hospitalized?"

"No. I don't plan to. They'd only worry. I'm fine now."

"You feel 100-percent normal?"

"Well," she hedged, "I do seem to get tired easier. Like today, I took a nap. But aren't *siestas* common in South America?"

"Yes. The heat and humidity drain our energy down here. So many missionaries return from furlough feeling energetic and gung-ho, but in two or three weeks they're dragging again. I've seen it happen and heard others talk about it, too. So, set a slower pace for yourself here. Brazilians do. They take *siestas* in the middle of the day when it's hottest."

"How was your Sunday-school class today?"

"Only six kids. But we did fine. I saw you heading out this morning with the Addisons. You went to First Baptist?"

"And then to the Hippie Fair and the *Avenida Restaurante*."

"I see the sparkle in your eyes. My guess is it's not for the church or for the food. You liked the crafts?"

"I could have spent another hour looking around, and lots of money if I'd had it. But then, again, I could paint most of it myself if I took the time."

"You could stay here another year when your time is up."

"Oh yeah, my parents would love that idea. They almost didn't let me make this trip. Maybe I should have gone to college across the continent instead of an art school near home right after high school. Then they would have gotten used to the empty nest a couple years ago."

"Do they write to you?"

"Every week. Mom tells me the news and asks a dozen questions. Dad adds a few lines at the end."

"Do your brothers live near them?"

"Two of them are within an hour's drive but in different directions. The third one is in the next state. They visit Mom and Dad regularly with their wives and kids to liven up the place. But I don't think you walked over here to discuss my family."

"I wondered if you'd like to watch several of us fly R.C. planes in half an hour. Kristy shows up when she hears the motors. We usually attract a number of spectators. And then I thought I might finagle the other meal you owe me. It doesn't have to be anything special. Even sandwiches would do."

"Forgot to go grocery shopping yesterday?"

"Me? Forget? I just never fit it into my schedule between all those dates. I'll have to go tomorrow."

"I guess I can rustle up some grub."

"Don't sound so thrilled. Makes me feel unwanted."

"Poor boy."

Keith stood. "See you in 30 minutes at the airstrip?"

"If I've finished writing this letter. Otherwise, just drop in later. I'll get something ready."

After he left, she stared at the door. *Watch out, Dani. You could fall fast for him. But he belongs with Maggie. That's what everyone says.*

So why was he asking her for a meal? He could go eat with Maggie.

Dani chewed on the end of her pen. And then she sketched a tiny Cessna 206 in the lower right-hand corner of the stationery and continued her letter.

EIGHT

"Where were you?" Keith asked.

"Over by the hangar." Dani flipped two pancakes and turned the sausages in the other fry pan.

"Smells good." He sniffed appreciatively. "Why didn't you go out on the field? I would have let you fly my sailplane."

"Too many people." She carried plates and silverware to the table. "I hope you weren't set on eating sandwiches tonight."

He gave one of his dazzling smiles. "As long as it's food, I'm not particular. I bet you've never flown a model plane. I wish you had let me know you were there."

Her wayward heart beat faster. She forced her voice to sound calm. "Yours was the yellow plane?"

"That's one of mine. I own three: two sailplanes and one regular. Did you see Tommy's red and white Sundance?"

Dani nodded and poured more batter into the pan. "I also saw Kristy fly it. She did a nice job."

"Her motto seems to be 'anything Tommy can do, I can do.'"

Dani giggled. "I think you're right. And one of these days she may try to add the word 'better.' How about getting the syrup out of the fridge?"

"You're putting me to work? If I help now, then no washing dishes."

"Afraid of getting those calloused hands in hot water?"

The banter continued throughout the meal. Talking with Keith was so easy. All she had to do to hold her own in conversation was pretend he was like a brother.

Keith forked another pancake onto his plate. "I read in the paper that BR-316 is going to get some *lombadas*."

"*Lahm-BAH-dahs?*"

He roared with laughter. "No, Dani. *Lambada* is a Brazilian dance, and, may I add, a risqué one. *Lombada* is a speed bump.

Several pedestrians have been killed or injured along the stretch between the grocery and the seminary. The speed bumps are supposed to slow down the traffic."

"Do I detect a note of sarcasm?"

"They'll put in a few teeth-jarring hills, but drivers will still make it up to 70-K or more in between them. I'll be surprised if it does any good."

"Seventy-K?"

"Kilometers. Remember, we use the metric system here. One of these days the States will join the rest of the world in using it."

"Don't hold your breath, buddy."

"I won't." He carried his plate and glass to the sink. "Hey, cute flowerpot." He lifted from the windowsill a small pot on which she'd painted a design. "Going to sell pots, or were you thinking of planting something in this?"

"The latter. I need an object lesson for two verses I read."

"Which are?"

"Colossians 2:6-7. I haven't memorized them yet." She snagged an index card lying on the sill and read, "'Therefore as you have received Christ Jesus the Lord, so walk in Him, having been firmly rooted and now being built up in Him and established in your faith, just as you were instructed, and overflowing with gratitude.' I like the 'firmly rooted' part, and I certainly need the 'being built up in Him.'"

"We all do. Thanks again for supper."

After Keith left, she washed and dried the dishes, put them away, and silently went over the conversation. *Friendship— nothing more, nothing less. Accept it and be happy, girl.*

Roy Davis called Dani into his office Monday morning after prayer meeting. "I've spoken with Deyse Castelo, a Christian woman who teaches elementary Portuguese at A.I.S. She has agreed to give you Portuguese lessons one hour a day until school begins in August. She can start today at 3. You could take her back to your apartment or use your office."

"Thank you. Even though my schedule is getting fuller as translators line up for future books, I do need to learn some

Portuguese. So far I can greet someone and count to 100. Period."

Deyse was a pleasant, middle-aged Brazilian. She understood English but told Dani to use only Portuguese. She taught the alphabet, colors, and clothing. Dani repeated the phrases umpteen times until her mouth felt sore from forming unfamiliar sounds. Each day they reviewed first and then added new words. Dani tried to imitate Deyse, but her grins from time to time let Dani know her accent was amusing.

In her spare time Dani completed Keith's pastel and set it aside on the closet shelf. What type of frame should she buy for it?

She began a pastel of the blue macaw—not in his cage but on a tree branch with some green leaves and spidery fuchsia flowers to balance out the royal blue of his body and wings. She was working on it one evening when Keith dropped by.

He set her I.D. card on the table. "I thought you might like to have this. Your mug shot, remember?"

"You mean I've been here a month already?"

"Yes. And your friend at the police station asked about you."

"He did? How nice," she said wryly. "I'm surprised he let you bring the card to me."

"He recognized me. Wow! That's gorgeous," Keith said, pointing to the pastel of the macaw. "You could frame it."

"I intend to, Mr. Kelcey."

"I can't believe how good you are. You're only 20. You have a long career ahead of you. You could sell your pictures."

"Stop right there. Yes, I suppose I will someday. But right now I draw for the mission and for my friends."

"Think you could spare some time Friday night to go bowling with Maggie, Ruth, and me?"

"I'm not very good."

"Is that a yes?"

She met his gaze and arched an eyebrow. "It's a maybe."

"I'll pick you up at seven."

Dani did go with them Friday night. While Keith was up to bowl, Maggie whispered, "Save next Friday night for a surprise birthday party."

"For Keith?" she whispered back.

Maggie nodded.

Dani would have to find the right frame for the pastel, and fast. She had no idea where to shop for it. Saturday morning she confided her dilemma to Jeni. Eric and Jeni drove her downtown. On a narrow side street they finally found a frame shop, but she found nothing suitable, so they continued on to several other stores.

"I'm afraid I don't understand." Eric's tone indicated his exasperation. "What's been wrong with all those frames?"

Dani's gaze roamed over the frames displayed on the wall of yet another store. "Size or coloring. The frame must enhance, not detract from, the picture. There! That's it!"

Jeni asked the price and translated to Dani.

"Ouch. I can't afford it, even though it's just what I need."

"Don't appear too eager," Eric cautioned. He bargained with the storeowner until the man named a price Dani could afford. He took the frame down, dusted it, and wrapped it in a large sheet of brown paper. Dani paid the stated number of *cruzados*, and the trio left, tired but triumphant.

On Sunday Dani went to church with Maggie and Ruth. Ruth shared her hymnbook with Dani. She whispered that parishioners who wanted one had to buy a copy from a bookstore downtown. Dani couldn't read Portuguese well enough to sing but tried looking for the few words she knew. She did recognize the tunes to two of the hymns and one of the choruses yet didn't feel free enough in this church to sing softly in English.

Maybe by the end of her year in Belém she would understand some simple songs and a tiny bit of the sermons. Staying awake was difficult when she didn't know what was being said. And the room felt terribly warm.

"Why does learning a new language have to be so difficult?" she asked on the way home.

"If we'd learned it as kids, it wouldn't have been," Maggie answered. "Children soak up what they hear and imitate it."

"I've been here 15 years," Ruth admitted, "and still have so much to learn. Those who live in Brazilian communities pick it up quicker."

"I wouldn't be brave enough to live off the center," Dani said, "even if it would help me learn Portuguese."

"You're staying only one year, so there's no need," Maggie pointed out. "Just make do with enough words to buy groceries and ride the buses."

"I guess you're right," Dani conceded. But somehow just "making do" didn't sound acceptable.

Monday morning Dani started drawing for the Addisons. They wanted illustrations for a book of Indian folk tales they were producing. During the week Dani drew a man with a bow and arrows, Indian women cooking by an open fire or grinding rice, another *açaí* tree, canoes, baskets, and several other pictures. She loved the work.

Each weekday morning she passed Gilda's office. Gilda, exuding cheerfulness, always dressed neatly in bright colors with lots of jewelry. Dani smiled and greeted the secretary, who did likewise. However, Dani was handicapped from forming a friendship by not knowing the language.

A copier machine sat in the foyer, accessible to all. Whenever Keith copied flight sheets or reports, he'd step into Dani's office and ask, "What are you drawing now?" And then he'd look over her shoulder, "Wow!" being his favorite comment.

"You must expand your vocabulary," Dani teased. "Perhaps take English lessons . . .." She blushed as it triggered a memory.

"Speaking of, has Kiko phoned you since the date?"

"Once. Last week. He said he'd heard I'd been sick and that he was terribly sorry. Then he asked for five minutes worth of help with his cassette lesson."

"Only five minutes?"

"Yes, sir. I didn't tie up the phone long. And I believe Kiko got your point. I did, too. I assure you I've learned my lesson."

"Are you happy here, Dani?"

She blinked in surprise, and stammered, "W . . . what makes you ask that?"

His hazel eyes searched hers. "Just wondering. No one else has asked you? They should."

"Why? I'm here to do a job. I'm doing it the best I know how. Happiness has nothing to do with it."

"But we should all make sure you adjust well and feel content. If you feel homesick or hate Belém, you'll leave. We'd all be out one great artist. So we should do what we can to make you feel at home."

Dani tapped his chest with the eraser end of her pencil. "I am not into psychology, but I assure you I'm doing fine. Please go back to copying, Sir Kelcey, so I can get my work done."

He retreated to the door. "I can take the unsubtle hint."

The next day Dani took a break from the Addison project and went to the *Bosque* with the Holmans. Dani had been curious about the square block of jungle ever since Keith had pointed it out. To make the outing more fun for Kristy, her parents had let her invite Tommy and Mary Davis also.

The group walked along the sandy paths, stopping at ponds containing alligators and fish and at various birdcages. The kids ran around and climbed the stone fort built to play in.

Dani finally sat on a bench with her sketchpad and pencils while the others continued their walk. She wanted some pictures for her file in case she might need them for illustrating a book sometime. She sketched a parrot, a toucan, and some hibiscus. When the Holmans returned, she was ready to leave.

They drove to a small restaurant off *Almirante Barroso* that served food typical of the region. John ordered a couple of bowls of *tacacá* and several plates of *vatapá* to split between them. The kids weren't terribly excited, but they ate the food.

Dani took only a few mouthfuls. "I don't think I'm hungry."

Rebecca laughed. "At least you can say you've tasted them."

"What's in them anyway?"

"The *tacacá*—the soupy mixture—consists of boiled *manioc*, tapioca, shrimp, and spices. The *vatapá* contains chicken sauce with various spices. It's served over the rice."

Dani made a wry face. "I guess I'd never make a good Brazilian."

"At least not someone from the state of Pará," John said. "Most of them love these dishes."

"How long would I need to live here for that to happen?"

"Fifty zillion years," Kristy cut in.

The adults chuckled.

"I suggest you keep an open mind—unlike my daughter— and let your tastebuds adjust gradually to Brazilian spices," Rebecca said.

"Can we get some pizza now, Dad?" Kristy asked wistfully.

Dani silently echoed her sentiment.

The pastel was framed and rewrapped in the brown paper from the store. Dani had painted little sailplanes on the paper first to make it look like gift wrap.

She felt nervous about the party. How would Keith react to being surprised? Would he like her gift?

Eight people stood around the A.I.S. poolside shelter, where Maggie had set up a small grill with hamburgers cooking on it before she left to get Keith. Rebecca and Ruth placed bowls of chips, rice, beans, and powdery *farofa* on the table. Jeni waved a towel over the food to keep flies away.

John and Eric were speaking with a Brazilian couple. Ruth took Dani's arm and led her over to them.

"This is Anita and José Cabral. He's a pilot for Varig airline on their international flights."

Dani gave the proper Portuguese greeting but didn't catch their response.

"Dani's had only a few Portuguese lessons," Ruth explained.

José switched to English. "We hear you are an artist. We'd like to see your work sometime."

"José and Anita are Christians," Ruth added.

"Great. How did you meet Keith?" Dani asked.

"Pilots gravitate toward one another. We have a special air about us," he joked. "No, really, it's because we're both Christian pilots. I like to talk with Kelcey about flying and about faith. I don't have many friends with whom I can talk about both."

"Shh," Jeni warned. "I hear them!"

They stood against one wall of the shelter and fell silent as they listened to footsteps draw nearer.

Keith said, "Someone's having a cookout. Sure smells good. Maybe we could invite ourselves."

Maggie and Keith stepped around the corner.

"Surprise! Happy birthday!"

Keith laid one hand on his chest. "Don't scare an old man like that!"

He walked around the circle, greeting each person. Anita kissed his cheek, and José gave him a hug. Dani assumed such actions must be cultural.

The hamburgers weren't quite ready, so Keith and José jumped in the pool and swam lengths. When they got out, Keith picked up his beach towel. He walked over to Dani and shook his head, flipping water drops onto her.

"Don't you swim? The water's great. Or are the women waiting until after supper?"

Dani would have been blind to not notice his physique. Two of her brothers were athletic, but Keith had them beat. With all those muscles, her original estimate of his weight was probably 10 pounds low. She forced her mind back to his question. "I swam at 5 this afternoon. After aerobics."

"The food's ready," Maggie announced.

The meal was delicious. Dani sat with Ruth, Eric, and Jeni at one table. The others managed to squeeze around a slightly larger table. The men ate several servings before Maggie carried over the dessert. The chocolate cake was decorated with small, plastic, party-favor airplanes. Twenty-eight candles were spread out over the top to make it more difficult for Keith to blow them out. Maggie had included two trick candles, which kept relighting. Keith finally plucked them from the cake and dumped them into a cup of water.

Maggie placed some of the presents on the table. The large candy bar was from Ruth. John and Rebecca gave a Belém T-shirt, while Eric and Jeni gave Keith a coupon for a homemade meal at their house. José stood, walked around the far wall, and returned with a case of orange soda, one of the bottles sporting a red ribbon. Keith seemed pleased with each gift as he joked and thanked the givers.

"Did you want to go next?" Maggie asked Dani.

"If you don't mind, I'd rather be last."

A brief flicker of annoyance showed in Maggie's expression. She slipped Keith an envelope, containing two tickets for an upcoming concert.

Nothing subtle about that, Dani thought. She masked her emotions and retrieved her gift from behind the wooden box of pool supplies. By its size and shape it obviously was a picture. She handed it to Keith and returned to her seat.

He turned the gift over and back. "I like the paper."

"Open it!" Rebecca directed. "We're dying of curiosity."

"We can't let that happen, can we?" Keith laughed.

Dani watched him carefully unwrap the pastel. She knew he expected it to be the blue macaw. He was so stunned he didn't even say "Wow!" for once.

"Let's see!" Maggie begged.

He turned it around and held it up. There were "oohs" and "aahs" and appreciative gasps. For a moment his gaze met Dani's across the tables. "You even drew in the grease streak," he said softly.

She felt an electric current pass between them and held her breath.

"What a wonderful picture!" Maggie broke in. "Such a good likeness. I bet your parents would love to have it."

Keith gave her a strange look. "Dani gave it to me, Maggie. And I intend to keep it."

NINE

School began the second Monday of August. It signaled the end of Dani's formal Portuguese lessons. She still knew very little but hoped to study more on her own.

At the end of prayer time several days later, Dani hesitantly asked, "Does anyone have a cassette player and language-learning tapes I could borrow?"

"I just fixed an old, discarded player," Conan replied. "You're welcome to it."

"Brenda has tapes she's no longer using," Tammy said. "I'm sure she wouldn't mind if you use them. I have the key to their house, so I'll get them later today."

"Thanks," Dani said. "I want to learn to speak Portuguese."

"Determination is half the battle." Tammy patted her arm. "See you this afternoon."

Two Api Indians showed up on the center. Olivia and Bob Martin were delighted to see them. The Martins settled them in the language-helper house so the men could help translate for a few weeks, sell the artifacts they'd brought, and buy supplies to take back to their village.

Olivia approached Dani. "Would you have even an hour a day to help us for the next two weeks?"

She hated to say no. "My schedule's pretty full," Dani responded. "But what do you have in mind?"

"One of the reading books we're working on is about Api festivals. We'd like to have illustrations. The men use body paint, feathers, and beads in different combinations and designs for each festival. Both of these men participate in the dances and can describe their dress for each one. We have photos of only three of the 11 festivals, so we need to get the other eight. I thought maybe you'd be able to draw the men while they're at the center."

"Sounds interesting—something I'd love to do. Any possibility that I can work after supper?" Dani's only other choice was to give up aerobics and swimming for the next two weeks, but she wasn't going to offer unless she had to. She needed the break and the exercise that hour afforded after sitting and drawing for hours.

Bob and Olivia discussed the daily schedule with the two men and approved the evening session. After supper Dani went to the Martins' house, which was next door to Keith's. The men were already sitting at the picnic table on the screened porch.

"Dani, meet Chori and Domini."

She smiled. The men grunted an acknowledgment. Dani flipped open a new sketchpad and pulled out some pencils.

"We'll start with the Toucan Festival." Bob translated his sentence into Api. The Indians nodded and began talking. The translation process went back and forth.

Dani interrupted, "Do all the Api men have similar facial structure? These two could be brothers, but they're not."

"Most of them do look alike," Bob conceded. "There's been a lot of inter-marrying in the tribe. All the men are built short, thick, and solid."

Dani started sketching as Bob continued asking Chori and Domini questions, then telling Dani their replies. Olivia joined them when she finished her work in the kitchen. She showed Dani some toucan feathers, several necklaces, and a loincloth. She described how the men wore them.

An Indian in loincloth appeared on the sketchpad. Chori leaned over and picked up a pencil. He drew lines down the chest and arms, indicating the body-paint design. Chuckling inwardly, Dani sat back and let him work.

Domini continued speaking. Then he stood and danced. He lifted his arms skyward and moved his head up and down. Dani made a mental note to redraw the man with his arms raised.

Chori finished the body paint and started on a headdress but gave up and laid the pencil down. Dani nodded, took up her pencil and drew in some feathers. Chori shook his head and spoke. Bob told her what to correct.

An hour and a half later Dani closed the pad and stood. A thought had been tickling her brain. "Bob, give Chori some paper and pencils. I think you'll be pleasantly surprised at what he draws."

The next night Dani laid two sketches on the picnic table. Domini and Chori discussed them. Chori pointed to the one where the Indian's arms were raised.

"That one," Olivia said. "But you need to add feathered anklets." She walked inside and brought back a pair. She laid them on the table.

Domini wrapped them around his ankles. Dani sketched them in. The men grunted approval.

"Ask Chori if he has a picture to show us," Dani prompted.

The Indian reached down the front of his T-shirt and pulled out a paper, crudely done except for the intricate body paint. He had erased and tried again and again to draw the hands, feet, and face. The paper was almost worn through in those spots. But he deserved praise for the attempt.

"Very nice." Dani smiled. "Tell him to keep practicing. He'll make a good artist if he keeps drawing."

"Wouldn't it be wonderful to have the Api illustrate their own books some day?" Olivia enthused. "The people would be even more likely to want to read the stories."

"It would be nice," Bob agreed. "Chori wants us to do the *Manioc* Festival next."

Domini rose and showed some of the dance steps. Dani picked two and drew rough sketches of both.

"Which one should I sketch in more detail?" she asked.

The men conferred. Domini placed a grubby finger on the left one. They described the jewelry and headdress for the dance.

For the next two weeks Dani spent her weekday evenings at the Martins'. Several of the festivals incorporated facial masks, which Chori drew. Dani showed him how to do shading. He caught on quickly.

One evening in the second week as Dani started home, she passed Keith on the sidewalk. He'd been jogging and glistened with sweat.

"Hey, Dani! How's it going? I hardly ever see you anymore——except from the other side of the prayer-meeting room."

"I'm staying busy."

"Maybe too busy? I hear you're moonlighting for the Martins."

She shrugged. "I'd be drawing pastels at home if I weren't at their place."

"Speaking of pastels, I hung your picture. Want to see it?"

Should she? She'd never been inside his place. Curiosity won over convention. "Sure. Just for a minute, though."

His apartment was larger than hers. One section of the main room sported a sofa and easy chair. The pastel of KCT hung in a prominent place on the paneled wall above the sofa. On another wall hung three R.C.'s. Off the kitchen was a screened porch and a red hammock stretched between two hooks. Against the far wall a long wooden table was strewn with balsa wood and Monokote.

"Except for the work table, you keep things pretty neat."

He grinned ruefully. "Fatima was here today to clean and cook. She's the one who keeps it neat, but she's not allowed to touch that table."

"Well, I'd better go."

"Would you like a soft drink first?"

"No, thanks. You mean you haven't drunk the whole case yet?" Dani teased.

"Nope. I drink the stuff sparingly."

She turned toward the door.

Keith laid a hand on her arm. "I really like the pastel. I was so surprised at the party I don't think I said more than a brief thank you."

You said more with your eyes. At least, I thought you did. But then Maggie claimed your attention. Dani cleared her throat. "I'm glad you like it. Good night, Keith."

"Are you going to the volleyball games tonight?" Debbie Addison asked Dani one Friday as they passed on the sidewalk.

"First I've heard about it."

"The girls' team is playing a tough team from the nearby subdivision. Brazilians love to play volleyball. When we're done, some guys get together and play a few games."

"Maybe I'll drop by and watch a bit," Dani said. "Are you enjoying your classes?"

"Yes." Debbie hesitated. "Do you know Richard?"

"Richard who?"

"Helms. He's a junior. He, uh," she dropped her gaze to the sidewalk and rubbed the tip of one sandal along a crack, "has a crush on you."

"He what? I don't even know him!" Dani's indignation softened when she glimpsed a hint of yearning in Debbie's eyes. "He must be about 17, right? I'm almost 21. I assure you I won't do anything to encourage him if I do meet him."

"You won't?"

"I promise. So how can you attract his attention instead?"

"Dye my hair brown and get a curly perm?" Debbie joked.

Dani chuckled. "I'm sure you'll think of a better way. See you later. I will plan on watching some volleyball tonight."

The school gym was "air-conditioned" in the sense that many of the cement blocks were constructed with square holes in them to allow for ventilation; the cement floor tried to keep things cool as well. Dani had never been here before. Some parents and students, including Kristy, were seated on the far side of the room, but most spectators stood along the wall closest to the double doors.

The girls were halfway through their second game when Dani arrived. Unfortunately, they were losing. She stood with the group near the door.

"Evening, Miss Dani. I'm Richard Helms."

She grimaced at hearing Richard's voice but returned the greeting with a frosty "Hello."

"I haven't seen you at a game before."

"No. Debbie invited me to watch tonight."

"Do you play?" Keith asked from over her shoulder.

She jumped slightly, even as she felt relief that Richard moved off to join his friends. "Not since junior-high P.E. class when I jammed my right thumb and couldn't hold a pencil for a week. I had to do homework left-handed and skip drawing while it healed. An awful experience. Painful, too. I haven't touched a volleyball since."

"Too bad. Volleyball is more exciting than bowling."

"The way I bowl, it wouldn't take much."

Keith grinned. "Remember, you said that, not me."

"Yes, you're off the hook."

The A.I.S. girls rallied and won the second game. The teams switched sides and began the third game. Some young Brazilian men arrived and stood outside talking and laughing. Keith went out to join them.

When the girls finished, the guys took over, Brazilians on one side, and five high school guys and Keith on the other. The play was much more intense. One of the Brazilian's spikes looked like a cannon ball fired at close range. Vicious.

Keith was good. When he served, he tossed the ball up and did a jump serve. Dani's mind took a snapshot. She tucked it away for a future sketch, which was how she drew many pictures when she didn't have time to actually sit and sketch the subject before it moved away.

The Brazilians were at least 20 years old. This put the kids at a disadvantage. Debbie had been right about Brazilians loving the sport. They were in top shape and looked like all they ever did was play volleyball. And could they jump!

The A.I.S. team was doing amazingly well against them. They were down by only a few points. Dani joined in cheering for them and applauding the good plays.

Between games Kristy skipped over. "Guess what? Someday I'll play on the girls' team. I'm already learning in P.E."

"Great! How's school going for you?"

"Fine. I like science and P.E—and music and art. Recess is the best, though. We get to play foursquare and tetherball. Mom said you drew a neat picture of Kelcey and his plane. Can I see it sometime?"

"Keith has it in his apartment. You'll have to ask him."

Kristy tugged her arm, pulling her down. She whispered in Dani's ear, "See that Brazilian in blue shorts and a black shirt? He's been watching you between plays. His name is Neto. He plays good. He lives beyond the wall. In fact, most of these guys live over there."

"Do they play in the gym often?" Dani asked.

"Whenever they can. They'd play every night if we let them. But they're not allowed unless they're invited by some of our guys."

"How much longer will they play?" The gym was hot; Dani was tired.

"They often take a break after the third game. Then they play again, but I have to go home to bed after the first set."

When the first three games ended, Dani turned to thread her way out of the gym between all the latecomers who blocked the door. Someone touched her arm; she looked back into the smiling face of the young man Kristy had pointed out. Two other players were with him.

He spoke in Portuguese. "Good evening, *Senhorita*. You're new here. My name is Neto."

Her mind slowly digested the words. She wanted to just walk away. Where had Kristy gone? The child could have gotten her out of this mess without Dani having to rack her brain for the right words.

"Let me introduce my volleyball friends." Keith suddenly stood at her left side. "This is Neto, Osmar, and Miki. I had fun, guys. See you later." He cupped Dani's elbow and made a path through the crowd at the door.

Keith had managed to get away without telling the guys her name. Hooray! Twenty yards down the sidewalk she pulled her arm away. "Mind telling me why you did that?"

"Because you needed rescuing. Just like with Kiko."

"I don't see the connection. I accepted a date with Kiko because I thought he was your friend. But I'd never been introduced to those guys. I was trying to think of an acceptable snub in Portuguese. I had absolutely no intention of encouraging their attention."

"Nice to hear."

"I told you before I've learned my lesson. All I was doing was standing there watching the games. I was even cheering for A.I.S. I barely even looked at them other than noticing how well they played. I did nothing to make them think I wanted to meet them."

"You didn't have to. You're pretty, and you're new. That's all the encouragement they needed."

"I think I could have gotten rid of them. When are you going to let me fight my own battles? And why are you walking with me? Aren't you supposed to be playing three more games? Kristy said they'd play a second set. You don't need to walk me home."

"In case you haven't noticed, it's dark. I am going to see you safely to your door, Daniela Austin, so accept it and calm down. Then, if I want, I can go back for more volleyball. You could act a little more grateful for being rescued from those three wolves. You see, I know them. I don't think you would have gotten rid of them so easily."

She bit her lower lip and counted to 10. "OK, thank you."

When she cooled down later, she would be more appreciative. He had said she was pretty; that was some consolation.

They reached her door, and she took the key from her pocket. Keith held out his hand for it. He unlocked the door and handed the key back.

"Thanks for cheering for us." He turned and walked away into the darkness.

TEN

"How are you spending the holiday?" Keith leaned against the doorframe of Dani's office.

She didn't even look up from the light table where she was aligning a picture onto a computer printout in order to paste it. "What holiday?"

"Tomorrow. September seventh, Brazilian Independence Day. You mean no one's asked you to do anything yet?"

She patted the picture into place and rotated her shoulders to stretch them, a telltale sign she'd been at this job too long today. "No. I suppose I'll spend it drawing."

He moved into the room. "Uh-uh, young lady. You get a day off just like everyone else."

Dani cocked her head. "So, what do you suggest, sir?"

"Quite a few people are heading for the nearer beaches—Outeiro or Mosqueiro. But they'll be noisy and crowded." He watched a blush stain her cheeks. "You did bring a bathing suit, didn't you?" She nodded but wouldn't look at him. "Dani, what's wrong?"

This time she cut him a glance. "I . . . well, Kiko mentioned his family has a house at Mosqueiro."

The blush was too pronounced for that statement. He knew something was behind it. "What else did Kiko say?"

She backed against the table. Did she think her unconscious act put distance between her memories and the Brazilian? What had the guy said or done now?

"Keith, nothing happened. Let's just drop it."

With great effort, he did so. "OK. Tomorrow Júlio Cesar airport hosts a small air show. Five of the trainer planes will fly in formation. But if you've ever seen the Thunderbirds or the Blue Angels, this will be nothing in comparison. The military hangar will have displays open to the public. Then, after that, we could stop by the Municipal Art Museum. If it isn't open on holidays, I know the zoo is. And we can eat out. It'll be my treat."

"Don't feel you have to babysit me. Didn't you get invited anywhere?"

She put up a good front, but he could hear the wistfulness in her voice. "I could go with some people to the beach and get sick on fresh shrimp that's sold by the bucketful at the bridge to the island. The guys will play volleyball or soccer, if they have room to move around all the sunbathing bodies. Or a lawyer I know, because he owns a private plane, invited me to bring the date of my choice to his club for a bash, which I politely declined since there will be a lot of drinking, dancing, and loud music. By the way, you may want these tonight." He took a tiny plastic bag from his shirt pocket and tossed it to her.

She turned the bag over and frowned at the yellow contents. "What is it?"

He grinned at her bewilderment. "Earplugs. You haven't heard anything until your eardrums are jangled by Brazilian music. The neighbors play it very loudly all night, because they believe everyone wants to share in the merriment. The drunker they get as the hours pass, the louder the volume. Unless you can sleep through a tornado, hurricane, and earthquake rolled into one, you'll be glad for the earplugs."

"Thanks."

"I'm not exaggerating."

"I'll let you know tomorrow."

She wasn't buying it, but by 2 a.m. she would be thankful for his gesture.

"Getting back to possibilities for tomorrow," Keith continued, "someone might have a soccer game, but you're probably not into that. At least you don't know enough Portuguese to understand all the bad language you'd hear at the stadium."

"Could we continue this fairly one-sided discussion later? I must get this booklet finished today. Please don't feel you need to include me in your plans. I can entertain myself."

Why was she being so difficult? "You need a day off, Dani. I'll pick you up at 9 in the morning." He scooted out the door before she could decline.

Dani spent the evening listening to the music blaring from the subdivisions on either side of the center and completing the sketch of Keith serving the volleyball. Feeling a bit guilty, she tore it out of the sketchpad and laid it on the top shelf of her closet. She was determined no one should ever see it. "I do not have a crush on Keith Kelcey," she mumbled. "I just wanted to prove I could draw it."

Why had Keith insisted she spend tomorrow with him? Where was Maggie going that he hadn't gotten invited? While it rankled to be second or third choice in his plans, at least she wouldn't be alone all day. No one else had asked if she had any plans.

She did need the earplugs, but even with them Dani got little quality sleep. When Keith knocked on her door at exactly 9 o'clock, she was dressed but still trying to get in gear. "Care for some coffee?" Her question was punctuated by a wide yawn.

Funny, she hadn't noticed before just how deep the dimple on the right side of his mouth was. The crazy grin he gave her showed it off to full advantage.

"Did you enjoy the music?"

"No. And the earplugs didn't work," she grumbled, pouring two mugs full of the strong black liquid. "Have some. Guaranteed to curl your toes."

He opened the fridge as if it were his own, grabbed the milk container, and poured some into his mug. "Thanks. But they don't need it."

"So, what has my babysitter decided we're doing today?"

"Aren't we grumpy this morning?" he asked in a sugary tone. "Maybe I should feed you to the eels at the zoo. Instead, let's head to the air show. I couldn't get a car, but I'll hail a taxi if the buses are crowded. Indulge my whim to be around airplanes for an hour or so. Then I'll take you to see some art."

"You scratch my back; I'll scratch yours?"

A light flickered in his hazel eyes. She stiffened. What had she started?

But he merely said, "Something like that. If you have sunglasses and a hat, bring them."

She picked up her sunglasses, but when she reached for the bag with her sketchpad and pencils, Keith said, "Uh-uh. No work today. This is a hol-i-day." He emphasized each syllable.

"But—"

"No, ma'am. Do I need to let you read the definition of the word?"

She rolled her eyes, put some money in her pocket, and headed for the door.

He hailed the first bus at the bus stop. "We're in luck. Most people are still in bed."

"After dancing and drinking all night, it's no wonder they conked out for a few hours. I'm glad we don't have to throw money away on a taxi." She handed the collector a few *cruzados* and slid into an empty seat.

Keith paid his fare. He folded his tall frame into place beside her, his legs sticking out into the aisle. "Taxis aren't expensive here, not like in the States. If we do take one today, it won't break my budget. And I could have covered your bus fare."

She shrugged. "No need to."

They got off the bus at the intersection leading to Júlio Cesar and hopped on another bus for several blocks. Then they walked down several side streets that led to the airport entrance. Small children were playing in open doorways of adobe homes. The older ones were in the streets. All were clad in old, stained clothes. Dani stared at them in dismay.

"What's wrong?" Keith asked.

"I'm not used to walking through this type of neighborhood. The little ones seem to have no adult supervision."

"The older kids watch out for their siblings while the grownups sleep it off." As they turned a corner, a mangy mongrel snarled at them. Keith stomped his foot and yelled. It slunk away, still growling.

"That building ahead is S.E.R.A.C., the equivalent of the F.A.A. I renew my pilot's license there yearly." He took her into Bentes's hangar to see the planes, then into the military hangar where they walked around the displays, and he translated for her. Occasionally he stopped to greet someone he knew; he introduced Dani by first name only.

"You don't remember my last name?" she asked dryly when the third set of people moved away.

"With mere casual acquaintances, it's proper to give only your first name. Giving a last name gets too personal. Brazilians like their privacy as much as we do, which is why they would rather meet you for dinner at a restaurant than invite you into their homes until they really know you well."

"Have you been in any homes, then?"

"Doctor Farias's, the Cabrals', and my pastor's."

They stood in the shade of the building to watch the short demonstration by the five trainer planes. Leaving the grounds, Keith hailed a taxi.

As they rode downtown, Dani asked, "So, where's Maggie?"

"Didn't she tell you? She and Ruth went to a church picnic."

"And didn't invite you?"

"Actually, she did. But I don't know anyone at their church. I thought I'd bug you all day instead. I wouldn't want you to miss your big brothers too much."

"Wow, thanks."

"I thought 'wow' was my word," he countered. "By the way, you said it backwards." He paid the taxi driver and steered Dani to a sidewalk café, where he bought a small roasted chicken, fried potatoes, and bottled water.

"Are you going to let me pay half the bill?"

"Nope." At a small table with an umbrella he held out a metal chair for her. "I invited you on this excursion and said it was my treat, didn't I?"

"Just giving you a chance to change your mind."

He passed her a wad of thin paper napkins. "You'll find the chicken's a bit greasy but delicious." He pulled off a leg and offered it to her.

Dani hesitated. "We eat with our fingers?"

He grinned. "Picnic style."

"Or caveman." She took the leg and daintily bit the meat. "I hope the vendor has a ton more napkins. But this does taste good."

"I have to tank up before we see any art."

"If you feel the museum will be an ordeal, you don't have to take me there."

"I didn't say that. Of course I prefer planes, but even at airports I'd get hungry after a while."

The city was waking up as more people took to the streets. The Municipal Art Museum was located in an old house on *Avenida José Malcher*. The collection of paintings, which dated from the first half of the 20th century, was small. They didn't need long to see everything.

"Now what?" Dani asked. "Oh, look at that wall!"

Diagonally across the street from the museum was a mural on a stucco wall. In bold colors, it depicted urchins throwing rocks tied to strings at the mangoes in trees and trying to catch the fruit as it fell.

"You'll see that scene often during mango season," Keith said. "Kids even dash into the street in front of cars to grab a fallen mango. Or a car screeches to a stop, the driver opens the door quickly, grabs the mango, and drives off."

"You're kidding!"

He shook his head. "You'll find more murals as you get to know your way around. City officials have found it an effective way to cut down on graffiti. They get locals to paint the walls. In some plazas and schools they've had contests with the walls divided into blocks for the painters or school children."

"I'd like to see them."

They strolled to the zoo. Keith paid the entrance fee.

"Now I probably owe you another meal," Dani sighed.

"I won't turn it down, but you don't have to invite me."

"Can we go see the manatee? And the eels? And the parrots?"

He laughed. "Lead on."

At work the next afternoon, she sensed someone watching her from the doorway, and glanced up. "Oh, hi, Keith. I didn't hear you."

"Hi yourself." He looked over her shoulder at the bird she was inking in for a primer. "You never cease to amaze me."

"I'll take that as a compliment. Need to copy something?"

"No. Would you like to go with me to a concert at the *Teatro da Paz* tonight? José had two extra tickets, but his in-laws can't go, so he gave them to me. The Chamber Orchestra is performing."

"But what about M—?" She stopped short of saying "Maggie."

His hazel eyes darkened a shade. "Have you seen the *Teatro* yet? I think you'd enjoy the art work and architecture."

Dani could play it as cool as he could. If he and Maggie were at odds, it was her temporary misfortune and Dani's gain. "I'd love to go, Keith."

"I'll pick you up at 7:15. The concert begins at 8. I'll sign out the *Gol*." He left before she could blink, as if not giving her a chance to change her mind.

Dani stared at the empty doorway. She hadn't thought to ask about attire. She didn't own anything fancy for an evening at the theater. What should she do? She reached for the center phone by her desk and dialed. "Jeni, this is Dani. I need some advice. What would one wear for an evening concert at the *Teatro da Paz?*"

"A nice dress, not cotton. Or else an elegant pantsuit."

"If I were to go downtown right now, do you think I'd find something appropriate, yet inexpensive enough for my budget?"

"I can tell you haven't shopped here. Prices are high; the styles are not conservative. And, believe me, I've seen all the stores."

She would have to find—or phone—Keith and cancel.

"Dani, is this for tonight, or the weekend?"

"Tonight. So I'd better call it off."

"May I ask who asked you out?"

The question was logical. She took a deep breath. "Keith. Only because his pilot friend José gave him two tickets for the Chamber Orchestra."

"I see. Say, we're about the same size. Walk over and look at what I've got. I have a few nice outfits I save for special occasions or for the conference in Brasilia."

"Are you sure you wouldn't mind?"

"I wouldn't have offered if I did."

Dani turned off the lights, locked the office, and walked to the Raymers'. From the back of her closet Jeni pulled three outfits covered with plastic bags. The navy chiffon dress had a sweetheart neckline embroidered with white scrolls.

Picturing herself in it, Dani ran her hand over the material. "This one, I think."

"Go try it on in there."

Dani knew it was perfect before she walked out for her friend's inspection.

"Looks great on you," Jeni confirmed. "It's yours for the evening. Just be home before the stroke of midnight."

"Oh, thank you!"

When Dani had changed back to her own clothes, Jeni slipped the plastic over the chiffon once more. "Dani, be careful. I probably don't need to say it, but I'd hate for you to be hurt. Falling for Keith would be so easy for you, but you have heard he likes Maggie?"

"Yes. Maybe she had other plans for the evening and couldn't change them on such short notice, so he asked me. He's just being a big brother. He knows I haven't seen the inside of the theater, and he says I'll like it because I'm an artist."

Jeni walked her to the door. "Enjoy it."

"Thanks. I will."

Spellbound, Dani gazed at the ornate lobby of the Peace Theater, the enormous chandelier, and the white marble steps. Entering, they had passed four statues representing Music, Poetry, Comedy, and Tragedy.

Keith offered his arm; she slipped hers through the crook. They ascended the polished steps carpeted with a strip of red down the middle. At the top were two marble statues, which she didn't recognize.

Their seats were in the first balcony. Dani looked at the domed ceiling graced with another huge chandelier. Around it were fresco paintings: a cupid with a bow and arrow, women and children dressed in cloth strips looking at an easel, and a god whipping four horses pulling a chariot. The ceiling over the stage was painted olive green, with gilt rectangles breaking it into small sections. The maroon of the velvet stage curtain was repeated in the banisters of the balconies. Gilt and flowers adorned small lamps on the side walls, the wallpaper, even the doorknobs.

"What do you think?" Keith asked.

"Impressive, but I'd never copy it for my home."

He chuckled. "Why not? I thought you'd love it."

"Not my color scheme, but I can appreciate the work. Just painting the ceilings would be a major undertaking, somewhat like Michelangelo and the Sistine Chapel."

People began filling the nearby seats. Dani sat back, not wanting to embarrass Keith by gawking at the artwork.

Keith opened the program and silently read. Then he leaned toward her to translate what the orchestra would be performing and the names of the members. She shifted slightly closer to hear him better.

When he finished, she noted how people were dressed. She was pleased once more at her choice from Jeni's wardrobe. "You are stunning," Keith had said when he first saw her. His eyes had confirmed his words. She'd felt a glow spread from her head to her toes. Maybe he said the same to Maggie every date, but this evening was Dani's to treasure and enjoy.

He wore a navy pinstripe suit, so it appeared they'd planned to dress alike. Dani mentally sketched a pastel of them standing next to the white balcony door with its peach-colored frame. People would see it in a gallery someday and say, "What a striking couple."

Ah, Dani, 'tis a bad habit you have. Better erase that pastel from your mind. Jeni warned you not to get hurt. What had Jeni seen in her expression? Dani would have to be a lot more careful to conceal her feelings.

A gong sounded. She arched her eyebrows and looked at Keith.

"The program will begin in a few minutes," he explained. "As you may have noticed, it's already a little after 8."

"Punctual, huh?"

José and Anita Cabral slipped into the seats next to Keith. Both were elegantly dressed in black. The Brazilian pilot leaned forward and grinned at them. "We just made it."

"So I see," Keith retorted. "Good thing you're not checking in to captain an international flight."

"I always arrive early for them. Nice to see you again, *Senhorita*."

Dani smiled. "Thank you. And thank you very much for the tickets."

The house lights dimmed. The Chamber Orchestra members walked onto the stage and took their places amidst polite applause. A man spoke a few minutes. The maestro took his place and raised his baton. For the next 40 minutes Dani was lost in the various pieces they performed.

"Do you like the music?" Keith asked, rising as the rest of the audience exited for intermission.

She stood also. "They're very good."

"Would you care to walk down to the lobby again—stretch our legs a bit?"

José and Anita were already moving toward the aisle. "We're headed to a room to one side of the lobby where paintings are displayed."

Dani smiled. "You sure know the right thing to say to get me moving."

"Lead on," Keith said.

The oblong room was crowded, but they managed to see a few paintings. Some were abstract; others were very daring in subject matter. Several times Dani blushed; Keith noticed.

"*Carnaval*," he said in disgust.

"What's that?"

He looked at her as if debating how to explain. "*Carnaval*— the three days right before Lent—is like the Mardi Gras in New Orleans. People give in to all their sinful desires because as soon as Lent begins, they're supposed to be good all the way through Easter. You don't want to go downtown or watch TV those three days."

He tapped José's shoulder. "We've seen enough of this, my friend."

"I agree." The pilot steered his wife through the crowd and out into the lobby once more as Keith and Dani followed.

Keith looked miserable. "I'm sorry, Dani."

"It's not your fault. But I do prefer the Hippie Fair art."

His lips curved in a gentle smile. "You like to make classic understatements."

They all drifted back to their seats. Keith casually draped one arm across the top of her chair. She fought the temptation to lean back.

"Will you join us after the concert for coffee or a late dinner?" José inquired.

Keith gazed down at her, eyebrows raised. "Would you like that?"

"I don't think I could eat another dinner, but coffee would be nice," Dani replied.

He turned to his left. "If you two haven't dined, feel free to chose a restaurant. We'll just meet you there for some coffee."

José named a four-star hotel. Dani sucked in her breath, but Keith merely nodded.

The second half of the concert lasted 40 minutes also. Once again the music was lovely. They joined in the hearty applause.

The hour was late by the time they bid good night to the Cabrals outside the restaurant. On the drive home Keith said, "Tomorrow I fly to Yabewa to pick up Ben and Brenda Tatum. You didn't get to meet them after the conference. You'll like them a lot. They're fairly young—no kids yet—and are fun to be around. An Indian man is joining them on the center for a few weeks."

"I'll meet them tomorrow afternoon?"

"No. I'll stay overnight. Ben's not the world's best fixer-upper, so they asked me to repair some things in their village house. We'll be back Saturday afternoon."

"I wonder if they'll want me to draw anything for them."

"Undoubtedly. I think every translator in Brazil would stand in line for your sketches if they could. Belém's fortunate we got you first."

"Yes, I'm so popular."

By the light of the dash she saw him grin. But he changed the subject. "Where are you going to church now?"

"Well, I don't have any particular church."

"Have you stopped going?"

"I . . . yeah, I guess so. I went to several, but it was such an effort to smile and pretend I could understand what was going on. I just don't know enough Portuguese to make it worthwhile. I've been staying home the last few weeks to read my Bible and pray."

"My kids would love to have you back to draw for them. How about this Sunday? I don't have a vehicle signed out, so we'd have to ride the bus. They're not bad on Sunday mornings."

"What's the lesson on this time?"

"Timothy—from boyhood to pastorship."

She could see a few possible sketches in her mind. Going with him would be better than sitting in her apartment. "OK, I'll go."

"Great. I'll even throw in lunch and a walk through *Ver-o-Peso* market. Have you been there yet?"

"No. Lunch? Just for drawing a Bible picture? I get the good end of this deal."

An annoying urchin was trying to sell them fruit. Keith watched Dani shudder at his nearness.

He spoke briefly to dismiss the lad and then took Dani's arm and steered her toward the wall by the water's edge. "See those large ships anchored in the Guajará Bay? They wait for space at the docks so they can unload cargo."

She shaded her eyes with one hand and looked. Her other hand clutched her shoulder bag containing sketching equipment.

She wasn't quite as pale as she'd been two minutes ago. "Are you getting tired, Dani?"

"I'm not used to so many people. And the smells here . . ."

"Fish, rotting fruits and vegetables, and stale sweat don't mix well in the heat, do they?"

Her nose wrinkled before she said, "No. Thanks for getting rid of the boy and the shirt salesmen. Why did they follow us through the market?"

"You looked interested in the shirt with the parrot painted on it. So word went down the line that the dark-haired foreigner wanted a shirt. Figuring you wanted a different color or size and hoping to make a sale, they showed you 20 possibilities. Once you show interest, it's a game to see who'll win the sale by giving you the best deal or offering you the exact item you want. You have to be firm and say '*Obrigada*' if you want them to go away. Otherwise they think you're playing the bargaining game with them."

"I'm glad you've got my money in your jeans pocket. I almost couldn't hold on to my art bag."

"Maybe I should take you home. Or would you like to walk through the Hippie Fair before we go back?"

"Is it near here?"

"I see the sudden sparkle in your dark eyes. Near enough for a quick taxi ride."

They walked out to the road. Keith hailed a taxi.

"Feels good to sit down," Dani murmured.

"I wish you'd said something sooner. We could have stopped in a café for a soft drink. Or are you ready for something more substantial?"

"No way. Lunch at the Japanese restaurant was quite filling." She laughed. "If you keep trying to confuse me with different countries and cultures, I'll never learn Portuguese and figure out what the pastor or the Sunday-school kids are saying."

"You're doing fine. But if you want to learn faster, you could join me at the Sunday-evening services, which are less formal. We sing choruses."

"Perhaps, but not today. My mind is boggled."

Scores of people milled about the sidewalk by the Hippie Fair, making it difficult to see the crafts and displays.

"Last time the fair wasn't this crowded," Dani bemoaned.

"Probably because you were here earlier in the day." Keith again took her arm so they wouldn't get separated.

"Oh!" Dani exclaimed. "Look at that highly polished redwood apple. My mom would love it. One of these days I should start buying souvenirs for my family and friends."

"What's the rush? You've got a whole year."

"Might be wiser and easier on my budget if I bought one or two gifts each month."

"Put that way, it's a good idea. Do you want your *cruzados*?"

"Yes."

She bought it. The woman wrapped it in newspaper.

"Ready to go home now?" Keith asked.

Dani looked down the sidewalk at the booths. "Sure. But some weekend I'm returning to sketch this."

"A snapshot wouldn't work?"

"My sketches are my snapshots."

"I wondered."

The bus was crowded, so they stood in the aisle. Yet the driver kept stopping for more people. Dani gripped the handle on the side of a seatback and braced her feet. Keith held the metal rod above their heads. He watched her eyes close and her knuckles whiten as they approached the dangerous curve. The bus tilted, throwing her against him. He put an arm around her waist. The bus righted itself; passengers breathed a collective sigh of relief.

"Defied death one more time," Keith murmured in her ear. The emotions washing across her face concerned him: anger, fear, and panic. "Are you getting sick?"

She shook her head.

Then he figured it out—claustrophobia. And they were still more than six miles from home. The person seated next to where Dani stood got up and squeezed into the aisle. Keith pushed Dani into the seat and inched into the place she'd vacated so he could guard her from more jostling. He leaned over her, his hand on her shoulder. "Look out the window and take deep breaths."

She momentarily obeyed him. But then her eyes closed, and she nibbled her lower lip. Was she praying? He began beseeching God on her behalf, too.

Two miles before their stop, the bus was still crowded, though not quite as bad as before. "We'd better start forward," Keith said. "Hang on to the back of my shirt; I'll clear the way for you."

They made it off the bus at the normal stop. Dani stood on the shoulder next to the four-lane highway they had to cross and began shaking.

Keith took her arm and gently pulled her onto the sidewalk. "You're all right now, Dani."

"I never want to ride a bus again!" Tears pooled in her eyes, but she dashed them away. "I'd rather walk or just stay on the center. That was awful!"

He tipped her chin up with one hand, so she focused on him rather than the noisy surroundings. "I prefer the wide-open feeling, too," he admitted, "which is probably why I like flying so much."

"You're not going to tease me for being silly, or berate me for being claustrophobic?"

He stroked her cheek lightly. "No."

She gradually stopped shaking.

"That's better," he said softly. He dropped his hand and took her elbow. "Let's cross the road and go home, Dani."

ELEVEN

Keith had been right about the Tatums: Dani liked them immensely.

Eric and Jeni Raymer left for a two-month stay in their village. While Dani missed her friend, Brenda Tatum stepped right in to fill the void Jeni's departure created.

Maggie and Ruth hosted a game night one Friday evening. They invited the Holmans and the Russells, who were teachers in the middle school, Ben and Brenda Tatum, Conan and Tammy Emery, Keith, and Dani.

They played Charades and several table games. As usual, Maggie did her best to occupy Keith's attention. He didn't seem to object.

What did Dani expect? Jeni had warned her.

During a lull, Jason Russell asked, "Does anyone know someone who could teach junior-high woodworking?

"Don't look at me," Dani laughed. "I can't saw or hammer a nail in straight."

"Keith could," Brenda remarked, "whenever he's not flying or fixing cars, stoves, radios, and everything else we keep breaking."

Everyone laughed.

The pilot drawled, "Stop volunteering me, or I won't have time to finish your 'fix-it' list before you return to Yabewa."

"How long will you stay in Belém this time?" Ruth asked.

"Probably five or six weeks," Ben answered. "We have a lot of checking to do with Saika, who's with us. We also need to keyboard quite a few texts and run off some copies to take back for further checking with other people in Yabewa."

"Dani, we've seen what you're drawing for others," Brenda said, "and we'd like to join your list of future projects. We have several story books that could be illustrated to make them more appealing to new readers."

"I'd be happy to draw for you," Dani replied. "Just stop by the office. We'll take a look at my schedule to see how soon I can fit it in. But don't be upset if it's not until the new year."

"You're booked up that far in advance?" Ben was astounded.

"She's in great demand," Keith affirmed before Dani could respond.

During the refreshment break, Dani wandered over to a table at the far side of the living room where a thousand-piece puzzle had been started. She studied it carefully and put a piece into place.

"Do you like puzzles?" In one hand Keith held a glass of punch; in the other a napkin with several cookies and a brownie.

"Somewhat." She nodded at the food. "A fringe benefit of game night?"

"My favorite part. I never refuse free treats—except when it's necessary for my health or sobriety. You should try these *brigadeiros*. Have you had any yet? Here, take one."

"The little chocolate balls? What are they made of?"

"Condensed milk, chocolate, and . . . I don't know; you'll have to ask Maggie or one of the other ladies."

"Mmm . . . they are good."

"No, you can't have the rest of mine. I'm greedy." He set his glass on the table. His eyes focused on the puzzle pieces, so Dani turned her attention back to them, too. She reached for a piece just as Keith reached for the same one. Their hands touched; she pulled hers away quickly.

"Well, well." Maggie's tone indicated she had observed the action. "Are you two helping Ruth with her puzzle project? She hasn't had much time lately. Maybe all of us should put some pieces together for her before we call it an evening."

Dani took a step away from the table. "I've already done several pieces. I think I'll try some punch." She retreated to join the Emerys and Holmans by the food. "Where's Kristy?"

"Babysitting at our house," Tammy replied. "I told her to phone if she had any problems."

"The kids will be fine," Conan reassured her. "They won't miss us at all. Kristy plays with them and reads them stories. They love it."

"Do you still do flight-following?" Rebecca asked Tammy.

"Yes. With only a preschooler at home now, it goes much smoother. I can respond to Keith's call-in immediately. I don't have to use the tape recorder to document his flight information as often as I did during the summer, when all three children were clamoring for attention."

"Have you ever listened to the flight-following, Dani?" Conan asked. "I bet you could draw a picture of Tammy with her radio."

"You're welcome to see what I do any time without feeling obligated to draw me," Tammy said. "I know how busy you are, but do drop in sometime, even if only for a coffee break."

"I'd like to."

"You know, Dani," Rebecca mused aloud, "if you ever wanted to make some money on the side, you could sketch kids' pictures and sell them to the parents. I'd buy one of Kristy."

Dani chuckled. "I'll tuck away that idea for the future. Especially if my funds are low some month."

Shortly thereafter, Dani walked home with the Tatums.

Brenda asked enthusiastically, "Would you like to go down-town on the bus with me tomorrow?"

"No, thanks!" Dani didn't want to go into detail about her utter dislike of that mode of transportation. "I need to catch up on some sketches for the Phillipses I'd hoped to finish today."

Dani closed her apartment door and leaned against it. *What am I going to do about Sunday?* Keith expected her to help with his class, but she could not face riding a bus. And he had made it clear he didn't use the car when families needed it. She got ready for bed and knelt on the small rug.

Lord, thank You for loving me just as I am and for letting me serve You here with the artistic ability You've given me. I want my life to please You. Thank You for friends and the good time tonight. And, please, Lord, don't make me ride a crowded bus again.

Saturday morning Keith dropped by Dani's on his way to the airport. She was sitting on her porch, sketching. He got out of the *Gol* and smiled.

"Hi."

Her cautious tone momentarily perplexed him. "Hi yourself. You should have stayed longer last night. We put in about 50 puzzle pieces."

"Sounds like you didn't need me."

"I didn't say that. Wow. Nice picture. You make the boy and his dog look alive. He's an Api."

"You can tell just by the features?"

"I've made many flights into different locations, so I can easily distinguish between each Indian group."

"I'm impressed."

"I could say the same about your art."

"So, you just stopped here to discuss my drawings?"

He didn't understand her wariness. He could try probing for the cause, or he could try using humor to defuse it. "Have you drunk your morning coffee yet?" Ah, the spark in her eyes rewarded his effort.

"Two cups. You're suggesting I need a few more? Or are you hinting that you'd like a cup?"

He wasn't going to admit he'd already had one earlier this morning. "Sure, if you're offering." He followed her into the apartment.

She poured two mugs and took the seat opposite him. "OK, what's on your mind?"

"I wanted to talk about Sunday school tomorrow."

She bit her lower lip but didn't answer.

"The Moores from A.I.S. drive a *Kombi* to church each week. They have room for one more, if you'd like to ride with them. I'll catch the bus and meet you there."

A flash of—regret?—appeared in her eyes, but she nodded. "Thank you. I appreciate it."

"The lesson is about Onesimus, the runaway slave. Can you think of a picture to draw?"

His question clearly amused her. "I'll read Philemon a few times and see what God brings to mind."

"I appreciate your drawing for my class so they have more than just a mental picture of the Bible story."

"I learn from it, too. When I have to pick one moment to freeze in time, I'm forced to look for the pivotal point of the story or the lesson God wants to teach us."

"I'm glad you're receiving some benefit, too." He glanced at his chronograph. "I'd better head on to work."

"On a Saturday? I figured you were going to the grocery because you were out of coffee and milk."

He smiled at her gentle teasing. "I have let supplies dwindle, because I'll be gone a lot the next two weeks. I've done most of the flight planning but want to check over the plane again. Thanks for the coffee. See you tomorrow."

He walked back to the *Gol*, glanced at her standing in her doorway, and drove away. Before he got to BR-316, he prayed aloud, "Lord, here I am again, asking for Your protection as I drive. I'm safer in the air than on the ground. But You provide all safety. You hold us in the palm of Your almighty hand. Thank You."

The *Kombi* was already packed with 11 people, but they squeezed in Dani. She still felt like a sardine—only in a more controlled environment than on a bus.

Keith's Sunday-school children liked her drawing of the returned slave standing before his master to be forgiven. While they played a game of "I Spy" after the lesson, Dani sketched one of the girls and one of the boys.

She sat beside Keith in the church service. Did people think they were a dating couple? How could Dani correct that misconception? Was it right to continue going to church with Keith when he liked Maggie? Dani spent more of the hour wrestling mentally than listening for Portuguese words she recognized or thinking over the text in her English Bible.

Mrs. Moore approached them as soon as the pastor said the final Amen. "We forgot to tell you we plan to eat out with the Tolands today. Can Dani ride the bus home with you this time?"

Dani stood in shock while Keith smoothly said, "Of course. Have a good afternoon. And thanks for bringing her."

When the woman turned away, Dani grasped Keith's arm. "No! I'm not riding a bus!"

He put his hand over hers and drew her away from the crowd at the back of the sanctuary. "Dani," he soothed, "we're heading out of town, not in. The buses won't be as crowded now as later on in the afternoon. Trust me. If I'm wrong, I'll hail a taxi."

Numbly she let him steer her out of the building. Traffic whizzed by as they walked on the sidewalk beside *Almirante Barroso*.

Keith led the way up the steps of the enclosed pedestrian bridge, then down the steps on the other side. "Do you know Psalm 56:3-4?" She shook her head.

"I learned the passage a few months ago when it was the kids' memory verse. Maybe you'd like to memorize it. 'When I am afraid, I will put my trust in You. In God, whose word I praise, in God I have put my trust; I shall not be afraid. What can mere man do to me?'"

Praying silently, Dani fought to control the panic. She took deep breaths and mentally scolded herself for the fear. The next thing she knew, they were seated together on a bus headed out of town.

"You can do it, Dani," Keith murmured in her ear. "The bus is definitely not as bad as last Sunday, see?"

"You think I'm overreacting, don't you?"

"No, I don't. I've had to conquer similar fears. Oh, not about packed buses but about bad weather springing up when I'm flying, or engine failures—things like that. Did I ever tell you I had a dead stick landing when I was 17?"

"No. Sounds bad. What is it?"

"The engine stopped. I was able to set the Piper down in a field without too much damage to it or me. But I didn't want to get into another plane for days. My dad guessed how I felt and made me get behind the controls. He was right, Dani. It was the best thing I could have done."

She self-consciously rubbed her sweaty palms on her skirt. "Thank you for sharing that. And thanks for not calling me immature or silly."

Keith stepped off the bus first and held out a hand to help her down. As the bus roared away, he squeezed her hand before releasing it. "You did it, Dani. And the ride wasn't so bad."

She took a deep breath. "I guess not."

They walked through a subdivision to get to the center instead of using the dusty road. The midday heat felt oppressive.

"I bet we get a storm later this afternoon," Keith commented, "which means no R.C. flying today. You still haven't tried your hand at flying my plane."

"I'd probably crash it, so consider yourself lucky I stay away."

"You'd do no such thing with me as your teacher!"

"What modesty and humility you display."

"Two of my best qualities."

"Bantering with you is fun. You remind me of home. My brothers and parents always joke around and say witty things."

"So, I'm like your brothers. I hope that's a commendation." He didn't wait for an answer but motioned for her to precede him through the narrow pedestrian opening beside the wider car gate at the entrance to the center. As they approached her porch, he said, "Next Sunday I'll be in a Poneraja village with the Phillipses. You can have a day off from drawing for the kids."

"And riding the bus." She hid her disappointment over his being gone.

"I asked one of the young people to teach in my place. She doesn't know about your sketches. The kids may tell her, though. Be prepared for your fame to spread."

She held up her right hand for a mock inspection. "I think I can deal with signing autographs."

Keith laughed and then sobered. "I'd appreciate your prayers. I'll have a lot of take-offs and landings and fly many hours over the next 10 days to pick up Christians for a four-day retreat in the central village and then fly them all back when it's over. Ned and Patti asked me to give a devotional or object lesson next Sunday. I'm not a preacher by any means. I haven't figured out what to say yet."

"You could share with them what you told us when you led prayer meeting—about God's thoughts for each of us being more than the grains of sand."

"I wondered if what I said got through to anyone that night. You were listening."

"Of course I was."

"The problem with using the same illustration is the shores on the Poneraja rivers are mud and clay, not sand. But thank you for your idea. I do have to think of something meaningful."

"I'm sure you'll think of a relevant concept. I'll pray for you."

"Thanks, Dani. Draw a few pictures for me while I'm gone." He turned and walked away.

Dani watched until the sidewalk curved, taking him out of sight but most definitely not out of mind.

TWELVE

Ten days had never before seemed so long. Dani filled them with sketching. And praying. She'd started a new habit of praying silently as she worked.

Brenda Tatum visited her office one day. "Where's the long waiting list we need to sign?"

Dani smiled. "Tell me what you have in mind. I'll see how to fit it in."

"Saika tells delightful stories. We'd like to make them into a reading book and have you illustrate it. He told a story about the flight to Belém and drew a picture. I thought you might like to see it."

The penciled sketch of KCT looked like a boat with wings, about the drawing level of a first-grader. "Why did he draw it this way?"

"Because the Yabeja people call Keith's Cessna 'the sky boat.' They have no other way to describe it. To them the airplane is a type of boat, which moves through the sky instead of water."

"How interesting."

"Saika conquered his fear of traveling in the plane with us because he knew what boat travel was like and that he returned safely to his village after paddling down river. So we told him the propeller on the sky boat would paddle us safely through the air to the big city and in a moon and a half take him back to his people."

"Our inventions must be frightening to Indians. 'A moon and a half'—an interesting way to tell time. I've never thought about months that way. Is this the only book you'll want me to draw for?"

"Oh, no. We'd love to have you draw for our primers, too. So you can add that to your 'to-do' list also."

"How nice to be in demand," Dani joked, penciling *Yabeja Stories/Primers* on her January calendar. "For drawing village scenes, I'll need to see photos or rough sketches of your people."

"Well, we could take you to Yabewa for a week or so. Then you could see it all yourself. You haven't gotten to visit any village yet, have you? Let me talk to Ben about it."

"Wait a minute. I'm a city girl. I don't even like camping. I'd rather draw from photos."

"We live in a house, not a tent. Sure we rough it a bit, but nothing drastic. You'd have fun. I'd take good care of you and do all the translating for you. And the people would love to watch you draw."

"You're so enthusiastic, I just might consider it. But don't get your hopes up."

After Brenda left, Dani sat deep in thought. She imagined eerie sounds and pictured jungle foliage, snakes, and bugs. Could she deal with a village visit? No. But she admired the translators who did it all the time.

She resumed drawing Indian women weaving mats. But the seed had been planted in her mind. For the next several weeks she mulled it over from time to time, wondering if she could survive seven days away from civilization. If she went, she'd have the chance to see some interesting sights and draw them firsthand. The idea began to take hold in spite of her fears and doubts.

In the evenings, she started another pastel—this time of Kristy. Rebecca Holman had indicated she'd love to have one. Her birthday was approaching.

Keith returned from the Poneraja village, but Dani didn't get to see him. As soon as he completed a 100-hour inspection on KCT, he succumbed to a malaria attack and spent the weekend in his apartment. The young woman had to teach his Sunday-school class again and spared Dani another bus ride.

Monday at aerobics Maggie said, "You're helping Friday with Field Day, aren't you?"

"Not that I know of," Dani replied. "What would I do?"

"Ann, the P.E. teacher, always counts on us singles to clock races and measure distances. Even some parents get drafted for part of the day. Let me sign you up. We won't do aerobics

Friday, but we'll get plenty of exercise measuring distances and chasing after hyper students. Then next week is mid-semester break."

"I'll have to check with Roy about helping on Field Day."

"He'll say 'yes.' Everyone joins in, even if their kids are grown up and gone."

Field Day was a big social event. Work on the center ceased for everyone. Dani was given the job of measuring shot put and javelin throws. She felt so hot standing in the sun. The few times she took a break to buy a soft drink from the snack bar, she noticed both Maggie and Keith clocking races on the track in front of the high school, while her tasks placed her on the other side of the building.

What had she expected? She couldn't do anything about Maggie monopolizing his time between races, but she did want to find out how the Poneraja talk went. After all, he had asked her to pray for him. She was glad he was well enough to be out of his apartment but hoped he wasn't overexerting himself too soon.

Dani went home at lunchtime and took a cool shower. Most of the others stayed at A.I.S. to picnic together. She didn't attend the awards ceremony late Friday afternoon either.

That night she carried the pastel of Kristy over to the Holmans. She was surprised to find the Davises there as well.

"Good to see you, Dani," John welcomed. "What have we got here?"

Rebecca joined him at the door. "Hi, Dani."

"I didn't know you had company. I'll give you this and be on my way. Happy birthday, Rebecca." She handed over the unframed pastel.

Tears formed in Rebecca's eyes. "How absolutely gorgeous! I can't believe it. Thank you." With her free arm she hugged Dani. "How did you know today is my birthday?"

"Kristy mentioned it a few weeks ago."

"Please join us for cake. We're finalizing our vacation plans. Our families are sharing a beach house at Salinas for the next week." Rebecca held up the pastel for her guests. "Look what Dani drew for me."

Roy Davis whistled. Irene said, "A perfect likeness. Can I commission one of my kids?"

Dani smiled. "I suppose so. But I may not get to it soon."

"Mommy, can Dani go with us to Salinas?" Kristy begged. "Please, please!"

Rebecca exchanged a look with her husband. "Fine with me, honey," John said.

"Would you like to go?" Rebecca asked. "The house is big enough, as long as you don't mind sharing a room with Kristy and Mary."

Kristy had put her mother on the spot, so Dani knew she should decline. "Thank you, but I have to work."

"You've been working overtime and deserve a break," Roy interjected. "I think you're ahead of schedule, so a week off won't hurt."

"I can't be ahead of schedule when work is stacked up on my desk and more scheduled all the way through January."

He laughed. "The translators will find enough for you to do for several years, if we let them. They love your drawings. But, if you want to go with us, then why not? You could take some work with you, if need be, and sketch at the beach or at the house in the evenings."

Kristy must have sensed Dani was wavering. "Please, please. We slide down sand dunes. The beach is so wide, cars drive on it. We boogie-board on the waves. Please, please."

"If you're sure I wouldn't be intruding . . ."

Dani went home and packed for a week at the beach. She put pencils, erasers, colored pencils, and two sketchpads into her shoulder bag. She phoned Keith to let him know she wouldn't be at church Sunday, but he wasn't home. Probably out with Maggie. So she phoned Brenda and asked her to relay the message.

Saturday morning the group squeezed into a packed *Kombi* and headed down the highway for the three-hour ride. Dani resolved to focus on her companions rather than on the tight fit, but she whispered to Kristy, "Why do we need all this stuff?"

"The house just has furniture and a few dishes. We take our own fans, hammocks, sheets, and all our food. Mom says it's too expensive in Salinas to buy anything but bread."

"Because it's on a peninsula and is a tourist trap," Tommy added from his spot next to Kristy. "I'm glad we had room for my Sundance."

"I did notice your plane wedged behind us," Dani teased.

They arrived at the beach house at 11. They quickly lunched on sandwiches and climbed back into the *Kombi* to head to Atalaia Beach, about eight miles out of town.

The beach was wide with beautiful, white sand. Sea gulls soared overhead. The waves looked just the right size. Small wooden buildings sat back several hundred feet from the water's edge. Some were open to sell refreshments.

John drove up to an unused building and parked. "We usually try to get close to this spot. With it being a busy weekend, I'm glad it wasn't already taken. The sand dunes rise up behind us, see? The kids'll want to climb them later."

The vehicle had barely stopped before the three kids grabbed their boogie-boards and tore down to the water. The two men began stringing up hammocks on beams. Dani helped the women set up a few lawn chairs and carried the cooler to the porch.

"We're so close to the equator, the sun is terribly strong here, Dani," Rebecca warned. "Be sure to use lots of sunscreen."

"Will I be safe walking down the beach? Or do I need someone with me?" she asked.

"You'll be fine, if you don't go far," Irene replied. "Just ignore the Brazilian guys."

Dani pulled off her T-shirt and let Rebecca smooth sunscreen on her back before she set out to explore the nearby vicinity. Two buildings down she watched a woman frying fish for some customers. Behind another place she discovered a pond, with a small duck floating contentedly.

Dani's swimsuit was a modest, turquoise one-piece with aquamarine and purple stripes diagonally across the front. She quickly decided to stop looking at people and what they were wearing and to concentrate instead on the scenery.

Dani didn't walk far before she turned back and joined the kids in the water. She swam for a while and then went back to the building and sat in a lawn chair. The men were lying in the hammocks snoozing; the women sat in chairs reading books.

"We love to vacation here and relax," Irene murmured. "No telephones, no pressing business to attend to."

"No school, no meetings," Rebecca added without looking up from her thick book. "I've been wanting to read this for months."

Dani laughed and pulled out her sketchpad. "I'll be quiet." She sketched the weathered building with their hammocks. Next she drew the kids skimming on the water with their boards.

The children exited the water to get a snack. They begged their dads to take them up the dunes while the moms poured more sunscreen on them.

"Tomorrow," Roy mumbled. "Plenty of time tomorrow."

They stayed two more hours and returned to the Salinas house for a simple spaghetti supper. After they washed the dishes, they all sat around the table and played a few games before they went to bed early. Dani had wondered if the girls would keep her awake talking, but they were asleep within minutes.

Sunday morning they sang choruses and prayed. Then Roy gave a devotional. Irene and Rebecca packed a picnic lunch so they could stay the rest of the day at the beach.

John led the kids and Dani on an expedition to the dunes. Roy and the two older women stayed behind at the same place they had claimed yesterday. Dani slipped and slid in the hot sand, but the view from atop the highest dune was worth the effort expended in getting there.

"Can we swim in Cola Lake, Daddy?" Kristy asked.

"Sure. Just don't tell your mom."

"Why do you call it that?" Dani inquired.

"Because it's black," Tommy replied, "and it's colder than the salt water. Makes you think you're swimming in cola."

They slid down the dune. The kids splashed into the murky water. Dani sketched a bush with light purple flowers. When she finished, the kids were ready to go back for lunch.

Returning to the ocean after they ate, the young trio noticed several jellyfish and rushed to tell the adults.

"We don't want anyone stung," Irene said, "so you'd better stay out of the water. Tomorrow you can wear jeans and long-sleeved shirts when swimming."

"What can we do now?" Tommy protested.

Roy laid his book on his chest. "With millions of tons of sand to play with, you don't know what to do?"

"We can make a huge sand castle." Kristy grabbed a pail and shovel and ran toward the water and wetter sand.

Mary and Tommy followed, Mary calling back, "Will you help us, Dani?"

"I haven't played in the sand for years."

"Time you did," Roy declared. "You're still young enough to enjoy it."

Dani pulled a T-shirt on over her suit. She worked an hour with the kids on a masterpiece castle. Irene took snapshots; Dani stored the scene in her mind.

"When can I fly the Sundance, Dad?" Tommy asked.

"Too windy today. Maybe tomorrow."

That evening Dani sat in a corner of the living room while the others read. She sketched an Indian woman grinding rice in a wooden pestle and another woman smoking fish over a fire.

Monday the kids wore their jeans and long-sleeved shirts into the water to protect themselves from jellyfish, should any be lurking in the shallows. Since it was a weekday, fewer people were on the beach. Dani walked, glad a lot of guys hadn't been staring or trying to catch her attention. She turned and started back for lunch but stopped in her tracks. Keith was striding toward her, not 50 feet away.

"Surprise!" he called.

Her smile lit her face. "You could push me over with a feather. What brings you here?"

"In case you haven't noticed, lady, this is a very popular vacation spot. The waves, the sand, the fresh sea air—what more excuse does one need?"

"And you're just in time for lunch, right?"

"Right. And Tommy is ecstatic that I brought my Gentle Lady to fly with his Sundance."

"I can imagine. He's been wanting to fly, but Roy's been putting him off. How did you get here? How long are you staying?"

"Doctor Farias lent me his *Kombi*. I can stay till Wednesday morning. I have to get back to prepare for a Thursday flight. The Sunday-school kids missed you yesterday."

She wished she dared ask if he'd missed her, too.

"Are you doing any sketches out here?"

"Beach scenes and some Indian ones for the Williamses." She looked at him quizzically. "Where are you staying?"

He grinned sheepishly. "I brought my hammock; I figured there'd be space to hang it in Tommy's room."

"You invited yourself?"

"Shocking, huh?" He laughed. "The Belém bunch is a close-knit group. The Holmans and Davises didn't even blink an eyelash when they saw me but just assumed I'd be joining you all."

During lunch Irene asked Keith, "Was it too far to go to Recife when you have to fly Thursday and Friday?"

"I'm sure you're aware Maggie and Ruth went there for the week," Rebecca added.

"Too long a trip." Keith took a bite of his sandwich, chewed, and swallowed. "I'm not much for riding Brazilian buses."

Dani almost choked on her soft drink.

Keith glanced her way. "I prefer air travel."

"Take us to the dunes, Kelcey," Tommy cajoled.

"Sure. You're going, too, aren't you, Dani?"

She hesitated, not convinced she should.

"You're one of us youngsters," Keith insisted. "We'll leave the 'old-timers' here to rest."

"Yeah," Roy muttered from his comfortable hammock. "Go while you still have the energy. You'll be one of the 'old-timers' like us before you know it."

"Go ahead," Rebecca urged. "Nothing's going on here. I can't believe how lazy I feel whenever I'm at the beach."

Five of them climbed the dunes and slid down to the lake. Keith waded in with the kids, but Dani stopped at the edge.

"What are you waiting for?" Keith asked. "The water is safe."

"Looks slimy." She dipped her toes into the cold murk. "What's in it?"

"Cola!" Tommy surface-dove, bobbed up near Kristy, and splashed her. Kristy immediately retaliated.

The next thing Dani knew, Keith stood dripping wet beside her, picked her up as easily as if she were a kid, and stepped into the water.

"Put me down!"

"Your wish is my command." He tossed her in. When she surfaced, sputtering, he was grinning. "You can swim, can't you?"

"Don't you think it's a little late to ask?"

"Kelcey could rescue you," Mary suggested.

Why did Dani have to blush? Of course, she could blame her pink cheeks on too much sun. "Rescue me? He's the one who's trying to drown me."

They swam for half an hour and then climbed the hot dunes and headed back.

Late in the afternoon the wind lessened. Keith put Tommy's plane and supplies in his vehicle. The two of them drove farther down the beach. The rest of the group walked down to watch them fly. Concealed by the dark glasses she wore, Dani's gaze followed the pilot's actions.

Keith used a high launch start for his Gentle Lady. On the sand he laid 30 feet of surgical latex tubing to which was attached 160 feet of fish line. He anchored the tubing end into the sand with a metal rod and stretched out the line by walking 30 steps beyond the end of it. He released the plane and ran back to where Tommy controlled the radio. The Gentle Lady soared into the blue sky and climbed higher. Keith timed the six-minute flight on his chronograph. They switched to the Sundance and repeated the process.

When it was time to leave the beach, Tommy and Kristy rode with Keith, carefully holding the two planes. The *Kombi* Dani was in reached the house before them.

Dani won the coin toss with Mary as to who got to shower first. Her hair was a curly mess again even after she washed it.

Irene and Rebecca had supper preparations under control. One reheated chili brought from home; the other cooked rice in a pressure cooker to save time. Mary had set the table and started the salad. Dani took over the task and sent the girl for her shower.

"Guess where we went?" Kristy whirled into the house.

"The equator?" her dad teased.

"No. To the lighthouse."

Keith and Tommy maneuvered their planes into the house and gently laid them in a corner.

"Kelcey took us up the red lighthouse," Tommy crowed.

"If you're trying to make Mary jealous, she can't hear you," Roy said. "She's in the shower. And you're next."

"Aw, do I have to?"

"Yes. Kelcey, make yourself at home."

"Thanks. I'll bring in my bag and hammock. And Tommy and I will wash supper dishes to earn our keep."

"We will?" the boy squeaked.

"Offer accepted," Irene said.

The evening ended with table games and laughter. Keith definitely added vivacity to the group. The kids obviously admired him.

When everyone finally retired, both Kristy and Mary were too wound up to sleep right away. They giggled and begged Dani to let them paint her nails and theirs. In their present state of emotions, she didn't trust them to not spill the polish.

"Maybe tomorrow," she hedged. "It's late. Let's try to get some sleep." She turned off the light.

"Have you ever been in love?" Mary asked two minutes later.

Could she fake sleep? No, that would be dishonest. "Love is more than having a crush on someone," she murmured, hoping the oblique answer would satisfy her. "When I was a teen I thought I was in love a couple of times."

"Do you think Kelcey's in love with Miss Maggie?"

The question was a knife thrust into Dani's heart.

Kristy sat up. "Of course. I think they'll get married in the gym so everybody can go to the wedding. And maybe she'll let all us girls in her class carry flowers or something."

"Naw, they'd get married in a church," Mary asserted.

"I hope they do it before school gets out in May. We're going on furlough. I don't want to miss out."

Someone tapped on the door. "Girls," Rebecca warned softly, "go to sleep."

The girls quieted. But Dani wondered how audible their words had been throughout the house.

She lay awake praying. *Lord, once again I bring to You my shattered expectations, my dreams. When will I ever learn?*

Tuesday they didn't climb the dunes. The longer they stayed at Atalaia, the lazier the adults felt. Dani was the only one not stretched out in a hammock under the roof. She was sitting on a chair merely watching people.

"Pleeease, Kelcey." Tommy and Kristy tried to tug him out of his hammock. "Don't just lie there. Swim with us."

"The water's too salty today," he mumbled.

Mary put her hands on her hips. "What a lame excuse."

Kristy poured a glass of water on Keith's chest. He shot out of the hammock, seized her before she moved three steps, and carried her, kicking and squealing, down to the waves. Tommy and Mary grabbed their boogie-boards and ran after them.

"You're not going to swim?" Irene asked Dani.

"Not right now." Dani snapped out of the malaise she'd felt since the girls' conjectures last night. She decided she'd enjoy this day while Keith was around and let the future take care of itself. She took up her pencil and paper and made a quick sketch of the hammock episode. She captured Keith's startled expression as the water poured from the glass.

After lunch, she joined Keith and the kids in designing a colossal sand sculpture of a Cessna 206. Irene took pictures. Then the quintet cooled off in the ocean. Keith and Dani tried boogie-boarding. She couldn't get the hang of it, but Keith was good. Laughing at herself, Dani handed the board back to Mary.

The wind calmed. Keith turned to Tommy. "Time for flying, but I want Dani to ride with me today, pal. Do you mind walking down in half an hour?"

Tommy looked as puzzled as Dani felt, but said, "OK."

Watching out for kids and sunbathers, Keith drove slowly.

Dani glanced at him. She liked the tan he had acquired in the short time he'd been here. He looked more relaxed, too. "The beach suits you."

"I wouldn't mind if Júlio Cesar and our center were close to Atalaia. You seem to like the place, too."

"I do. But I'm getting very little done; this is supposed to be a working vacation for me."

"My guess is you've accomplished much more than you think." Keith parked the *Kombi* and lifted the Gentle Lady from the back. "Here, hold this, please. I'll bring the line and radio."

Dani carefully carried the large sailplane. "I think Tommy could have helped you more. I don't know what to do."

"You're prettier than he is." Keith stretched out the line on the sand and returned to take the plane from her, handing her the radio instead. "Besides, you've watched me, and now it's your turn to fly this baby."

"Oh, no. I can't."

"I'll show you what to do." He attached the end of the line with its tiny yellow parachute to the towline hook on the plane. "I'll launch it; you control it."

"I haven't a clue—"

But he was pacing out the 30 steps. He launched the Lady and ran back. Dani held out the radio for him to take; he gently pushed it back.

"Move the controls like this." He stepped behind her and put his arms around her. His hands covered hers as he showed her which direction to turn the stick for each maneuver.

Dani's mind turned to mush. She tried to focus on the plane and what Keith was saying, but his nearness and touch sent her senses reeling. He could not possibly realize the effect he was having on her. She knew he thought of her as a kid sister. As far as he was concerned, she could be 9 or 10 years old. He'd probably helped Kristy the same way when she first started flying.

"Relax, Dani," he said over her shoulder. "You're tense. You won't crash it with me here guiding you."

They landed the plane on the sand 20 feet away as Tommy ran up. Keith let go of her hands and stepped away.

Tommy gave Dani a look that seemed to say, "Girls! Oh, brother!" He picked up Gentle Lady and carried it to Keith. "She's not going to fly my plane, is she, Kelcey?"

"No. But she did fine; don't you agree?"

"Only because you did it for her. I saw you. She's just an artist, not a pilot."

Dani exhaled. Good thing Tommy was the one who'd seen them; any of the others would have interpreted the little scene much differently.

Keith walked to the car to get the Sundance. He helped Tommy launch the plane. With the boy controlling the radio, Keith moved to stand by Dani. "Want to fly again?"

"I don't think so. I would have crashed without you—" She stopped before saying, "holding my hand."

"All you need is practice; you'd learn fast. I could help you with the landing, which is the tricky part."

"No. The others are almost here."

He looked at his chronograph and called out, "Five minutes, Tommy. You're doing great!"

The girls and their fathers joined them. Dani stood back to watch. She needed to sort through conflicting thoughts and emotions.

Lord, here I am again. Please calm my heart and help me not read too much meaning into what just happened.

THIRTEEN

The day Dani got back from Salinas, Keith stopped by. "You sure got tanner after I left," he commented.

"Kristy says I look like a Brazilian now. Too bad I can't speak like one to complete the image."

"Would you like to find out more about their customs and traditions?"

"Like what?"

"*Círio.* Tonight features a procession on *Avenida Magalhães Barata* ending at the *Basílica de Nazaré.* People carry on their shoulders a platform on which sits a festooned statue of Mary, the patron saint of Belém. Next to the *Basílica* is a fair with a ferris wheel, bumper cars, and other rides. The Tatums, Maggie, and a couple of high-school students want to see the procession. Ben signed out the *Kombi.* We have room for you, too."

Safety in numbers. Safety for her heart. "Sounds interesting. Sure, I'll go."

"Great. We'll pick you up at 7."

Dani was surprised when Keith motioned for her to take the seat next to Maggie. He took the front passenger seat of the *Kombi.* The students sat in back. Police had closed the avenue to traffic, but they finally found a place to park on a side street and made their way to the crowded sidewalk near the *Basílica.*

"Stick together, kids," Ben told the students. "If you get separated from us, we'll meet at the entrance to the rides when the procession ends."

"Same goes for big kids," Keith said as he walked between Maggie and Dani.

She felt a prick of irritation at his implication that she was still a kid. In less than a month she would turn 21.

People jostled others for viewing spots along the street and sidewalks, but they found a nice place from which they could watch the parade. They heard singing and chanting for 10 minutes before they saw the platform and the statue of Mary being carried down the wide street. Some people cried, sang, or prayed out loud to Mary, while others followed quietly behind the core group.

The procession moved down the street and into the plaza in front of the church, where a special shrine had been built for the statue to be kept the rest of the year. The crowd thinned as people dispersed around the plaza or to the fair for the rides.

"Dani," Keith said, "we're going now."

Maggie slipped her arm through Keith's. They walked toward the fair.

Last month Dani had held his arm at the theater. Well, at least she didn't have to watch them holding hands. She turned to the Tatums. "I should warn you I'm prone to claustrophobia. Sometimes when I'm in a crowded place, I fear I won't survive."

"We'll help you," Brenda assured her.

The *Círio* fair reminded Dani of the few county fairs she'd attended while growing up: same type of rides and games to play, and lots of cotton candy, hotdogs, and soft drinks. But everything was in Portuguese. Street kids walked around selling shoelaces of all colors printed with the words *Círio Nazaré*.

Dani watched the others toss rings onto pop bottles, ride the ferris wheel, and drive bumper cars. Her tolerance for the noise and confusion wore thin.

When Brenda stepped off the ferris wheel with Ben, she took one look at Dani and said, "Why don't we go sit in the plaza? Ben, you can stay if you want. Those kids probably need a bit of chaperoning."

Because no park bench was vacant, they sat on the grass. Dani breathed deeply. "Thanks, Brenda. I'd had enough of that."

"Me too. I don't care for fairs as much as I did when I was young."

"And you're so old now?"

"Nearing 30. One of these days we'd better start having children. The Yabeja women can't imagine why I don't have any. Most of their women my age are already grandmothers. Now that Ben and I are settled and have learned enough of the language, we want to begin our family."

"How young do they marry?"

"At 13 or 14. And always to a man who's at least 20. He has to prove himself to be a good provider first, or the girl's parents won't consider him."

"Sounds like a good idea. I haven't seen your pictures of the village yet."

"Once you do, I guarantee you'll want to visit in person. Have you thought more about going with us? We're delaying until the first part of November. Saika agreed to extend his time in Belém. He managed to send word back to the village that he's well and will return at the end of two moons instead of the original plan. If you go, we could arrange for Kelcey to fly back a week later to pick you up and bring in more supplies. Even with just Saika along, we can't take in as many supplies as we'd need for several months, so we're asking for a second flight anyway."

"You know, I still find it interesting that most people call Keith by his last name."

"You're hedging," Brenda challenged. "But if you need more time to say yes, I won't push for an answer now."

"I have no idea how I'd fit such a trip into my calendar, but show me the pictures first."

"Sure."

At 10 o'clock the group reassembled. Ben announced, "Iby's for ice cream!"

The kids cheered; Maggie and Keith nodded in agreement. At the small shop, the others ordered cones, but Dani declined.

"No ice cream?" Maggie asked. "We'll do aerobics tomorrow."

"I know," Dani said.

Keith was perceptive. "Thinking about the last time? The food poisoning was probably more from the potato salad than the vanilla ice cream at Cairú. To be on the safe side, pick a flavor one of us has already chosen."

"So I'll have company if I get sick again? No, thank you. I'm fine without."

A half hour later Ben stopped the *Kombi* in front of Dani's apartment. Keith looked over his shoulder. "Don't forget Sunday school tomorrow. I'll see you at the regular time."

She felt Maggie stiffen beside her but said, "Sure. Thanks for taking me, Ben and everybody."

At aerobics Monday afternoon, Maggie didn't waste any time before asking, "You're going to Keith's church?"

"Yes. I illustrate Bible stories for his class."

"Oh, I see." Her tone held a touch of jealousy, but she let the subject drop. When they took a dip at the pool later, she began discussing Fall Fest with Ruth.

"What is it?" Dani asked.

"An annual fund-raising event by the high-schoolers to earn money for gym, video, or other equipment," Ruth explained.

"Fall Fest," Maggie continued as she eased into the pool, "is the first Saturday night in November. The kids have picked a Western theme this year. They'll decorate the gymnasium and make booths or activities, like a cake walk or hay ride. Parents, friends, and many Brazilians attend. The kids haven't drafted you to help them draw backdrops and make decorations yet? Of course, most of them don't plan ahead."

"You think they'll want my help?" Dani asked.

"I'd bet on it—if I were a betting person," Ruth laughed.

That week Keith flew both the Williamses and the Phillipses out to their tribal locations. During her coffee break on Wednesday, Tammy invited Dani to hear how Keith radioed in checkpoints every 15 minutes or so. Dani watched Tammy write down all the information on a flight sheet. Tammy repeated everything on the two-way radio so Keith would know she'd heard.

"Did you understand?" Tammy asked when the radio was silent once more.

"No. It was in Portuguese. The voice didn't even sound like Keith's."

"You'd get used to his radio voice if you heard him all the time."

"Maybe. Do you enjoy flight-following?"

"The job is perfect for my situation. I can do housework, watch my pre-schooler, and still perform a necessary job for our center. Keith usually flies only 30 hours a month, so I regularly get days off."

"Speaking of work, I'd better get back to my office. Thanks, Tammy, for the coffee and cookies. See you later."

Friday morning at prayer meeting, Roy announced he had an official notice from the Indian Agency concerning artwork and books. "They have requested we get Indians involved in illustrating the books we produce. Our P.R. department assured them we'd be happy to cooperate. I'll schedule meetings with each translator left on the center to discuss ways we can fulfill this new obligation. I know it will affect your work, too, Dani, but just keep working on your present projects until I can meet with you next week."

Dani found concentrating on drawing to be difficult. How many of the projects stacked on her desk would be put on hold, or even scrapped? She might not be needed here much longer.

The Tatums phoned and invited her to supper. Joining them was better than sitting home alone. When Dani arrived, Saika was on the porch whittling a flute from one of the many kinds of beautiful wood found in Brazil. She nodded a greeting, which he returned. They sat down to eat stew and corn bread. Saika ate quietly.

"The Yabeja don't talk during meals," Ben explained, "but we told him our culture allows it. Don't feel badly if he acts like he's not here. We'll include him in our conversation after the meal."

"The announcement this morning was quite a shock," Brenda said. "You looked like someone dropped a brick on you, Dani."

"I almost felt like it, too. I had a tough time sketching today. Will what I've been doing ever get used?"

"Don't give up yet," Ben stated. "Let the Indian Agency look at your work. They'll want to use it, too. I predict all your sketches will be used many times in the years ahead."

"I was thinking," Brenda said slowly, "about translation workshops. We haven't gotten that far in our work; we understand just enough Yabeja so we can start the Gospel of Mark. But if the workshop idea could be used to get some of the Indians interested in drawing pictures . . ."

"You may have something," Ben agreed. "We could bring in a few men from each language group for a one- or two-week stay here. Dani could show them some principles of drawing."

"But how would I communicate?" Dani asked.

"Each translator would have to translate your words and ask you the men's questions," Ben replied.

"Why only men? Is it wrong for an Indian woman to draw? Or what if some of the children show promise?"

"A woman might have ability," Brenda said, "though probably not much time to draw, considering her responsibilities as a wife and mother."

"I don't want to put a damper on your idea, but what if no one is interested?" Dani asked. "Chori tried to draw when he was here working with the Martins, but he became frustrated. I know he could improve, though, if he'd only practice. But what incentive would there be for Indians to draw? I mean, do you think they'd do it just to see their sketches in some book?"

"We'd have to pay them to draw, like we pay them to teach us the language or to help translate God's Word," Ben stated.

Brenda leaned forward. "We could have a talent search. You know, a contest of some sort to see who shows promise. We could have children and adults draw for us. Then we'd decide which ones to bring here for further training. Each translation team could do the same if they wanted."

"Or we could generate interest in our village by taking you out there, Dani." Ben grinned wryly. "I know Brenda's been asking you to visit us. If you walked around Yabewa sketching the people, their natural curiosity would have them following and imitating you. We could pass out paper and pencils and see who has natural talent waiting to be discovered."

Dani leaned back in her chair, crossed her arms, and thought for a few minutes. Brenda looked liked she would pop from the suspense, but she kept silent. Saika finished eating his stew.

"My full calendar has been temporarily cleared with the new decree," Dani said, "so that excuse is gone. Maybe you could ask what he thinks."

Ben spoke to Saika, who nodded and answered.

Before Ben translated, Dani knew all her objections to visiting Yabewa were insignificant compared to the goal of seeing primers, story books, and Bible passages being read and enjoyed by Indians.

"Saika said, 'You fly in the sky boat. Teach us to draw nice pictures for our books. I like picture books. Sky-boat man showed me what you drew for him. You teach me. Then I can make my sky-boat picture look better so it will be in the book. My people will read and learn much.'"

Dani sighed. "I'll go."

Brenda looked like she wanted to jump for joy. Instead she quietly breathed, "Praise the Lord."

FOURTEEN

The school gym was a flurry of activity. Students kept calling Dani to check the decorations or give advice on drawing their backdrops for various booths. They had been at this for several hours already. Dani was bone-weary.

"Dani, is this the right shade of green for a cactus?"

"I can't get this steer to look right, Dani!"

"Does this look good enough for the Bank of the West?"

"This cowboy would like to speak with you, Dani."

Those last words broke through the tangle of sounds. From her kneeling position Dani looked up at Keith and smiled. "Hi, KCT Cowboy."

"That has a nice ring to it. Do you think you could take a break from chalking in the storefront and make time for lunch?"

"I didn't realize it was so late already. But, yes, I need a break." She stood, wiped her chalky hands on the sides of her jeans shorts, and walked beside Keith. They passed the booth nearest the door. "Debbie, that horse looks great."

"Thanks, Dani."

Outside, Keith said, "They'll keep you busy all day if you let them."

"But everything is still so chaotic. I doubt we'll finish by 7."

"Don't let them exploit you. The kids do this every year; they always wait till the last minute. But somehow the gym looks fantastic when the doors open to the crowd."

Dani bristled. "'Exploit' is a bit strong."

"I'm sorry." But he didn't sound very contrite.

"Where are we going? I live at that end of the center."

"My place."

She stopped walking. "Why?"

"Two reasons, Miss Inquisitive. The first is to eat lunch. I bought pizzas at the grocery. One's in the oven right now. I'll even have plenty left over for another day. The second is that none of the kids will be able to reach you by telephone or by running over to your apartment, because you won't be there. You can rest from the hustle and bustle for an hour."

Did she dare go to his place for a meal?

"Dani? What are you thinking?"

She resumed walking with him without answering.

"Are they making you work tonight, too?"

"They've talked me into sketching quick portraits for anyone willing to pay eight tickets apiece. The kids are making a booth for me in the far left corner. I told them I had to be out of the mainstream of activity, or I wouldn't be able to concentrate."

"So, it's not just crowded buses that get to you?"

Her eyes met his. "No." She didn't want to admit to him that, since her arrival in Belém, her claustrophobia attacks were more frequent than ever.

He held the apartment screen door open for her to enter. She glanced immediately toward the wall where the pastel hung.

Opening the oven door to check the pizza, Keith said, "Your picture will always hang in a prominent place wherever I live, Miss Austin."

"How did you know . . . ?" she sputtered.

He shrugged. "Sometimes I can read your expressions. Sometimes I can't." He set the first pizza on a breadboard on the table and poured ice water into two glasses.

She washed her hands in the kitchen sink and sat down beside him. Keith said the blessing. They munched in relative silence for a few minutes. Dani began to relax after the hectic morning.

"I hear you'll be on Tuesday's flight," Keith said.

"Yes, the Tatums talked me into going. I wonder, though, if I'll survive one very long week away from civilization."

He chuckled. "You'll be pleasantly surprised at some of the comforts they have. I rigged up a shower and a solar panel for them last year. They have to pump water from the well up into the shower reservoir once a day, but that isn't too difficult. They also have a small kerosene fridge and stove. The Indians are still trying to figure out those modern conveniences."

"I can only imagine how strange our ways seem to them. I've never flown in a Cessna before. I hope I don't disgrace myself and get sick on the flight."

"You'll be fine. Just be sure to eat breakfast—maybe toast and a glass of milk or cup of coffee—because flying on an empty stomach is worse than having eaten a little something. And try to relax. You're a very intense person, putting your whole self into whatever you do. Lean back and enjoy the flight. I'll write down a few scenic spots you can watch for."

"What Tammy called checkpoints?"

"Those, but also a few others. When did you talk with Tammy about checkpoints?"

Dani wished she didn't blush so easily. "I went to her place for a coffee break one day. She was flight-following you."

"If I'd known you were there, I'd have said hi."

"You don't sound the same over the radio. And I didn't understand the Portuguese."

He sobered. "Dani, I just thought of something. I never got to let you ride in KCT while I taxied it back to the Airclub, but you saw how small the 206 is when you sketched it. Will you be able to deal with having four other people with you in that amount of space? You'll be with Brenda in the middle seats, so I won't be beside you like I've been on the buses."

"Oh." She began mulling it over.

"With God all things are possible," Keith affirmed. "I did not want to imply otherwise, but you need to be aware of what to expect. You can pray for His strength and peace."

She took a deep breath. "I can't very well back out now."

"Brenda would be disappointed, but your well-being is more important than her feelings. However, you could look at it as a growing experience. Sometimes God puts us in what we consider impossible situations so we'll have to lean on Him."

"I know."

"So you won't be too surprised Tuesday, let me explain one rather strange aspect of pre-flight procedure. When I have all the baggage and passengers loaded in KCT, I have to check the center of gravity. I walk back to the tail and push it down almost to the ground. If I've loaded the plane correctly, the tail will rise back up when I let go. I'll try to remember to warn you just before I do that."

"All right." She wiped her mouth and set the napkin on the table. "Not saying you'd ever err, but what happens if you haven't loaded the plane correctly?"

He smiled. "I'd make everybody deplane and run laps around the airport until they weighed less."

"Uh, right. I can just see that. The pizza was delicious. Thanks for inviting me."

"You're welcome."

"I should probably get back."

He laid a hand on hers. "Nope."

Her heart raced, but she managed to ask, "Dishes first?"

Laughing, he removed his hand. "Not that either. You deserve a whole hour lunch break. I'm making sure you get it. Let's go see the new R.C. I'm building."

They stepped into the screened porch. The table was littered with balsa, Monokote, and a skeleton of a wing. The other wing, with its royal blue coat, was propped in one corner of the porch.

"I'm making another Electra Deluxe."

"Takes a lot of work, huh?" She bent to inspect the frame. "Do you always pay such attention to details?"

He moved closer. "No, I don't. I'm learning that women have a natural knack for details, while men have to cultivate and develop the trait."

Needing more physical and emotional distance, she took a step away from him. "Don't get philosophical on me, Keith. I'm just a simple artist. I haven't been to college like you, and Maggie, and others." Dani's eyes grew wide. If Maggie found out she had eaten lunch at Keith's, fireworks might occur. "I'd better get back to the gym."

He was studying her. "Only if you promise to walk slowly. You still have 10 more minutes of your lunch hour." He walked her to the door. "You're wiser than you think, so don't knock yourself, Daniela Austin."

"Thanks again for lunch."

"My pleasure. See you tonight."

The gym had been transformed into a Western town, complete with a bank where tickets were sold, a jail, a general store, and corrals. The high-school kids were dressed in chambray shirts or calicos, jeans, boots, bandannas, and cowboy hats. And they were only minutes late in opening the double doors to the crowd awaiting Fall Fest.

Dani had borrowed from Brenda a pink gingham skirt with a ruffly white blouse. She sat in her corner and watched people pour into the gym. Fear bubbled up inside. She took deep breaths and turned her back on the scene. She looked instead at her open sketchpad. She'd brought the small-size book because she was supposed to spend only five minutes on each sketch.

Her first customer was Mary, who simply said, "My mom wants a picture." She sat on a chair against a prairie backdrop.

Dani perched on a stool and did a quick sketch. When she finished, people were trying to peer over her shoulder. Five of them wanted to be next in line. She had to consciously ignore the panic. For the next hour she sketched steadily, taking no breaks. She managed to draw 12 faces. Several of them were Brazilians from the nearby subdivision.

Kiko showed up with a flashy date. Why had he ever noticed Dani weeks ago? They paid double the number of tickets for Dani to draw them sitting side-by-side. They were pleased with the sketch.

Tommy was next. He seemed to begrudge the five-minute gap in his evening of fun. And then two high-schoolers dressed in black grabbed Dani and led her off to the jail.

"Stop! What are you doing?" she demanded. "I'm supposed to be drawing!"

Paul shrugged sheepishly. "Someone paid extra tickets to have us put you in jail. Sorry, Miss Dani, but we have to do it."

Richard added apologetically, "Only for three minutes."

"No! I don't care how long it is."

When they closed the bamboo bars, the only other person in the square makeshift jail was the volleyball player, Neto.

She wanted to bolt. She rattled the bars. "Paul, let me out this instant!"

Surprisingly, the boy complied.

Fleeing the jail, Dani ran smack into Keith's broad chest. She looked up at him and could tell by the glare in his eyes that he had seen the incident that just took place. He grasped her arms to steady her. "You're all right, Dani. You can go back to sketching. The jailers won't take you again. And Neto won't bother you, either."

"Thank you," she whispered.

Her sketches that hour weren't nearly as good as the first ones had been. She had to force herself to concentrate and not give in to the shakes. Maggie stopped by to visit for a few minutes on her break from selling tickets.

The Tatums also stopped to watch. "You look tired," Brenda commented.

"I'm fine. I've had several nice compliments on this outfit. Thanks for letting me borrow it."

"Have you gotten to do anything except draw?" Ben asked.

"Oh, I was put in jail briefly."

"Which doesn't count. You deserve a little fun, too," Brenda protested. "Did you notice all the other booths have two people staffing them? The kids planned it so they could relieve one another."

"But no one else can do these sketches."

"Yeah, we know you're indispensable," she teased.

At 9 o'clock Keith showed up and stuck a "Closed" sign over Dani's booth.

"What's that for?"

"Just what it says, ma'am." His Western accent was amusing. "'Closed' means 'closed.' No more sketches. You've done your duty and then some. Time for some fun. No protest. That's right, ma'am. We're gonna do the Cake Walk. One of us is gonna win a cake or pie, 'cuz I'm hungry again."

He produced tickets from his shirt pocket and led Dani to the chalk circle drawn on the middle of the cement floor. They stood on two adjoining numbers and walked around when the music played.

"The chocolate cakes and other fancy ones have already been picked," Keith commented from behind her. "But what's left still looks appetizing."

The music ended. A number was pulled from a jar. A Brazilian was on that square and clapped his hands in glee. He picked a pie from the table. Only one cake and one pie remained. Keith gave the student in charge two more tickets, and they walked to the music again. This time Dani was on the winning square.

"Hooray!" Keith exclaimed. "Go for the cake."

"It's a bit lopsided. Looks like caramel frosting."

"At least it's edible."

"And you want to eat now, right?"

"The pizza we had at lunch is long gone, ma'am. Why don't we mosey on over to your place and cut this thing?"

"Sure. I'm ready to call it a day."

They passed the ticket booth on the way out the door. Maggie wasn't inside, or Dani would have asked her to join them. "Maybe we should ask Ben and Brenda to help us eat this."

Keith looked stricken. "I could eat most of this scrawny cake all by my lonesome, and you want me to share?"

She laughed. "All the sugar will probably make you sick."

"Sounds good to hear you laughing." Keith spoke seriously now, abandoning his Western accent. "Earlier tonight I thought you might go hysterical. I had a few choice words with Neto over his little trick."

"Oh, Keith, I panicked when they put me in jail with him. I didn't want to talk with him, I just wanted out."

"I know. I could see that. Well, here we are."

She unlocked the door and flipped on the light. Keith made a great show of placing the cake in the center of the table while she reached for a knife, forks, and two plates. When she sliced into the cake, she murmured, "Happy birthday to me."

"What? Today's your birthday? You're joking."

"This day was so hectic, I never even thought about it until now. I didn't receive any cards in the mail, but they might arrive Monday."

"Let me get this straight." Keith cocked his head, clearly bewildered. "Today is your birthday, but you just now thought about it?"

She made a face at him. "No need to advertise with neon lights. Really, it's no big deal."

"Isn't this your 21st?"

"Yes." She laid one slice on her plate and two on Keith's. "But I don't look it, do I? Everyone thinks I'm a kid. Maybe when I reach 50 or so, looking younger than my age will be advantageous."

"Twenty-one is special." Keith cleared his throat and sang "Happy Birthday" in both English and Portuguese. He clapped as he sang the latter.

Dani was giggling when he finished. "Oh, dear. I'm so tired I'm getting giddy."

"If I'd known what day it was, I would have bought you a gift."

"You did. The pizza and the tickets for the cake. So, I say thank you, KCT Cowboy."

He took a bite of cake. "How is the new Indian Agency ruling affecting your work? I forgot to ask you at lunch."

"Roy told me to keep drawing. Many of my pictures are being copied and put in a file. If the Indians don't catch on to the drawing idea, or the Indian Agency withdraws the request later, translators would be able to choose from among my pictures to illustrate any of their future books. Or else they can modify them to fit their particular group. You do know, don't you, that the Tatums plan to use my visit to generate Yabeja interest in illustrating their own books?"

"That's why you're going?"

"Part of the reason. Brenda thinks I should see at least one location while I'm in Brazil. She says she'll love having me there, and I won't create too much more work for her. But, I'm not so sure. She'll have to follow me everywhere and translate. I think she'll be tired of me after a week and ready to send me back in the plane."

"What if I forget to fly back to get you?" Keith teased.

"The Tatums will boil you in oil if you don't bring their supplies and get me out of there." Dani stifled a yawn. "Want another piece of cake?"

"No, thanks. I'm sweet enough for a few hours." He stood and carried his plate and fork to the sink. "Time for me to mosey homeward," he slipped back into his fake accent. "You've had a mighty long day, missy."

Dani stood. "I forgot my sketchpad and pencils. I'd better go back. And I probably should take down my booth, too."

"Let me do it. You look really tired. And you've put in so much overtime this weekend, you ought to have tomorrow off from my class and listening to a Portuguese sermon. Stay home and rest. I'll drop your stuff off as I walk by in the morning. How's that sound?"

She yawned again. "Better than I could have dreamed. Just don't tell my parents or the mission board I'm playing hooky from church."

"I won't." Leaning down, he brushed her cheek with his lips. "Happy 21st." He stepped out the door and called back through the screen, "Good night, Dani."

She managed to echo, "Good night." Her fingers touched her cheek in wonder.

FIFTEEN

Amazingly, Dani did fine on the flight to Yabewa. Brenda was the one who looked as though she would be ill.

"Are you OK?" Dani asked above the roar of the engine.

She leaned closer. "I've never gotten airsick on a flight before, but yesterday I found out I'm pregnant."

Dani clasped her hand. "Oh, Brenda, it's what you wished for. I'm so happy for you."

"I'll be happier once we're on the ground. I sure hope this doesn't mean morning sickness for the rest of the first trimester. I certainly don't need that in the village."

The flight lasted an hour and a half. Dani mentally checked off each spot Keith had written on her "things-to-look-for" list. The landing was as smooth as could be expected on a grass strip. She breathed a prayer of thanksgiving for the safe flight.

Keith got out the pilot's door. Ben scooted across the seat after him. Keith slid his seat forward and offered Dani a hand to climb out. "You fared well. No claustrophobia?"

"None. I actually enjoyed the flight."

"I'm glad. Brenda, you don't look like you're going to run any marathons." He held out a hand to assist her.

"Not today, Kelcey."

Ben was busy greeting the village men. Keith walked around the plane and opened the cargo door.

Saika, who had sat in the rear, exited from that door. His people gathered around and began chattering with him. He smiled and gestured with his hands as he answered their questions about his trip and the sky boat.

Some of the Indian women gathered shyly around Brenda, who greeted each one by name. Several women glanced at Dani, so she smiled. One rather young woman with a baby in a shoulder sling smiled back and then immediately looked down at the ground.

Keith unloaded the belly pod and took several boxes from behind the rear seats. "All done. I'll be on my way now. But next week I'll bring in the rest of the supplies and spend the night. You can start your 'fix-it' list for me, Brenda."

"Thanks. I will."

Keith shook hands with Ben and Saika. Then he turned to Dani. "Enjoy your week. We'll miss you in Belém." He looked at Brenda. "Take good care of her, huh? And yourself, too. I've never known you to be queasy on a flight before. You're not getting the flu, are you?"

"She's got the nine-month variety," Ben joked.

The pilot blinked and then smiled. He clapped Ben on the back. "Congratulations, pal. You, too, Brenda. Well, I'll see you all next Tuesday."

Indian men picked up the duffles and boxes. Everyone moved to the edge of the clearing, watching from a safe distance as Keith climbed into KCT and yelled, "Clear!" in Portuguese to warn everyone to stay clear of the propeller. The engine roared to life. Keith taxied to the end of the strip. In a few minutes the Cessna was just a small speck in the sky.

"Well, Dani," Brenda said, "let's trek the half mile to the village."

The rest of Tuesday was spent unpacking and being visited by all the women and children. Each one wanted to meet Dani and chat with Brenda, who looked like she needed to take a long nap but couldn't because the culture demanded she talk with each guest until they decided to leave.

The Indians repeatedly brought up one particular topic. Ben and Brenda clued Dani in as they ate a quick lunch during a short lull between visitors.

"Two Indians from some forgotten tribe showed up three weeks ago. One was very ill; the other asked for help," Ben said. "Their language isn't Yabeja but is related. Sasi knows some of what he calls 'the old talk.' He says his grandmother spoke that language. He learned from her before she died, but he'd forgotten most of it until these men arrived."

"The women are afraid of the tall one," Brenda added. "He's called Moju. The sick one is Zio."

"Jacaré, the chief of our village, sent word immediately to the Indian Agency. The agent visited for a few days. Apparently there's talk that the two strangers will either be relocated when Zio gets well, or our village will be asked to keep them. The agent thinks the rest of their tribe has died off."

"How sad." Dani could imagine how awful she'd feel if all her relatives died.

Later in the afternoon Dani swept out the cobwebs and dust from the small house. "I'm amazed I get my own room. Even a bed instead of a hammock. Impressive."

Brenda sorted through the canned goods on a kitchen shelf. "Luxury," she joked. "We're a one-star hotel in the jungle. Sheets and mosquito nets are stored in a barrel in my closet. Be sure to take the dust covers off and check for bugs under the mattresses before you make up the beds."

Dani shivered but did as requested. Fortunately, she found no bugs or spiders. If she had, she didn't know how she would have reacted.

Brenda placed a can of condensed milk into a pan of boiling water. "I'm craving *doce de leite*. It'll only take an hour to cook. We can have some on the bread we brought along."

"Better than pickles and ice cream."

She sighed wistfully. "Ice cream won't keep in our fridge."

"All the Yabeja women seem to like you a lot," Dani observed.

"I do have quite a few friends already." Brenda stacked more of the canned goods into her pantry. "But I'm concerned for their salvation—afraid someone will die before we know the words to tell them God loves them so much that He sent His Son, Jesus, to die for their sins. I'm so excited that Ben's going to start translating the Gospel of Mark while we're here this time."

"Do translators always start with Mark?"

"Usually. Because it's the shortest Gospel and has more action words—which are easier to learn when one is picking up a language—than abstract theological concepts."

"I admire you and the other translators for your dedication in the midst of primitive conditions and hardships."

"Dani, we're just doing what God called us to do. He's the One who enables us, just like He does for you in your job."

The two women went to bed as soon as Dani washed the supper dishes and Brenda put them away. Ben lit a kerosene lamp and stayed up to plan out the next day's work.

Dani awoke early to strange jungle sounds. Surrounded by the mosquito netting, she lay in bed praying. *Lord, I'm glad I'm safe inside a house. I don't know what this day holds in store, but You do. I'm both excited and nervous. Help me not to run ahead of You nor lag behind Your plans. I pray Brenda will get over the morning sickness quickly. Help me be a blessing to the Tatums and to the villagers. In Jesus' Name, Amen.*

After a simple breakfast, Brenda felt up to walking through the village with Dani; she greeted all the women and children in sight. Carrying sketchpad and pencils, Dani would have sat down and drawn several scenes if Brenda hadn't kept her moving on.

Brenda stopped by the young woman with the baby in the sling that Dani had noticed yesterday. "This is Moki and her daughter, who has no name yet. Yabeja don't name children until they reach their first birthday."

Moki spoke and pointed to the sketchpad.

"She says Saika told everyone about the pretty pictures in there. She wants to see them. He says you are here to teach the people to carve on the white leaves. She wants to learn."

Dani opened the pad and showed her several pictures of other Indian groups. These were extras which hadn't yet been put in the file in the office. One picture was of a mother and child.

Again Moki spoke and Brenda translated. "She asks if you will carve her picture with her baby."

"Sure. I'd love to."

"This is our opening, Dani. Let's sit on that log so you can draw."

Moki removed her baby from the sling and cradled her in her arms. This allowed Dani to see the face clearly. The cute daughter was plump and looked healthy.

A crowd gathered to watch and comment. "They are discussing what you're doing," Brenda said, "and what Saika told them. Most are skeptical that they could learn to carve on paper like you."

Dani finished the sketch, tore it out of the pad, and gave it to Moki, who held it against her chest and crooned.

"She loves it, Dani. She's saying 'thank you.' She will put it on a wall in her house."

Dani smiled. "What next?"

"Draw a village scene for them."

A detailed sketch of a home with a scrawny dog lying in front and a cooking fire off to one side appeared on the paper. People took turns looking over her shoulder as she drew. She consciously ignored their closeness and concentrated on sketching.

"We cannot carve like that," one woman told Brenda.

"Tell them I've been drawing since I could walk," Dani suggested. "Tell them some people here can learn to carve, if they will practice, just like they've learned to canoe, hunt, or weave baskets."

"Good idea. I'll pass it on." Brenda spoke in the strange-sounding language.

When Dani finished the sketch, an old woman stepped forward speaking in Yabeja and holding out her hand.

"She lives in the house you drew," Brenda explained. "She's asking for the picture for her wall."

Dani smiled, tore it out, and handed it to her. The woman looked pleased and nodded. Dani stood and stretched.

Brenda spoke again to the crowd. As they walked back to the house, she told Dani what she'd said. "We have white leaves and carving sticks for everyone who wants to try. Tell your men when they arrive home to eat. They can carve also. Whoever wants may visit my house after lunch and practice carving. Dani will look at each leaf and pick three or four. The people who drew them can carve with her for five days. After she leaves in the sky boat, they can teach others in the village."

"Do you think they'll show up this afternoon?"

"They'll show."

Two women, nine children, and five men tried out for Dani's class. In order to be fair, Dani sat in her bedroom while the Yabeja drew. Then she chose three pictures without knowing who had drawn them. Brenda asked their owners to step forward. Moki, Saika, and a man named Jabuti walked to the table where Dani sat.

Brenda held a small discussion with the three. Then she turned to Dani. "They ask for class to be held after lunch each day. Does that suit you?"

"Yes."

The next morning Dani wandered around the village sketching plants and village scenes. Children followed her; the mothers were busy with chores.

Near lunchtime she glanced up and gasped. Standing 15 feet away and carrying a five-foot bow was a solemn, imposing Indian dressed in a loincloth with feathers stuck through his nostrils and ear lobes and his body painted with *urucu* and coal. Around his chest hung a quiver of arrows. This had to be Moju.

Dani looked around the village. No woman or teen girl was in sight, only younger children. How strange. They were out weaving mats and stirring their cooking pots just a minute ago. Where did they go?

She closed the pad, stood, and walked back to the Tatums', resisting the temptation to turn around and look again at Moju. What a picture he would make. She must sketch him before leaving Yabewa.

The first class Dani gave was on simple objects and shading. She set a can, an arrow, and a small box on the table. After each student drew the items, she demonstrated shading them to show depth and lighting.

Her days fell into a pattern. She helped with cooking the meals and washing the dishes. In the mornings, always followed by most of the children who gestured or laughingly tried to make her understand their words, she sketched. This helped Brenda, who was able to rest or talk with the women instead of translating for Dani.

The afternoon class progressed from the simple objects to plants, hammocks, and canoes. Then they tried animals and people. Almost all the sketches by Moki, Saika, and Jabuti were on a second- or third-grade level. Dani kept encouraging them and pointing out ways to improve. "How long is my arm in comparison to how tall I am? How big is Jabuti's head compared with the rest of him? Is the dog really as big as the man in your carving?"

The students sometimes laughed at their mistakes, but they worked diligently to please her and improve their pictures. On Saturday Saika asked if they could draw the sky boat. She let them try.

"This picture is better than the one you drew in the city, Saika. When the sky boat returns in three days, look carefully at it to see how big the paddle on the front is compared to the body. How big are the wings? What about the windows? How would we show which way the sunlight touches the boat?"

In the evenings, after dishes were washed and put away, Dani sat outside until dusk to carve portraits of the Yabeja. She gave away each sheet to a pleased patron. Then, after a cool shower, she'd fall into bed with barely enough energy left to tuck the mosquito net under the mattress edges.

Moju has not shown up to be carved, she thought. *But what had he wanted?* In the back of her mind she held the snapshot pose of him for the sketch she knew she had to draw.

Several times each day she counted the hours until Keith's return, not admitting how much she missed him. She'd gotten used to catching glimpses of him at the morning and Wednesday-evening prayer meetings or when he drove past her apartment on his way to or from the airport. She puzzled over his behavior on her birthday. On the other hand, why indulge in wishful thinking? Keith liked Maggie. In his opinion Dani was a mere kid.

Sunday morning Ben, Brenda, and Dani held their own church service. Having only three people felt a little strange until Dani remembered Jesus' words in Matthew 18:20: "For where two or three have gathered together in My name, I am there in their midst."

They sang hymns, prayed, and read Scripture together. Ben shared his thoughts on Galatians 6:9: "Let us not lose heart in doing good, for in due time we will reap if we do not grow weary."

"I am often tempted to give up," he said, "when I see how long it's taking us to learn the language, or I think of the enormous task of translating the whole New Testament into Yabeja. But God wants us to be faithful with today and not 'lose heart' or 'grow weary.' He will give us the strength day by day. After all, getting His Word to the Yabeja is His job. We are merely His instruments in the process.

"Let us be encouraged, too, with the words of 1 Corinthians 15:58: 'Therefore, my beloved brethren, be steadfast, immovable, always abounding in the work of the Lord, knowing that your toil is not in vain in the Lord.'"

The last hymn they sang was "How Firm a Foundation." Dani pondered the words as she and Brenda worked on lunch.

How firm a foundation, ye saints of the Lord,
Is laid for your faith in His excellent Word!
What more can He say than to you He hath said,
To you who for refuge to Jesus have fled?

When through fiery trials thy pathways shall lie,
My grace, all sufficient, shall be thy supply;
The flame shall not hurt thee; I only design
Thy dross to consume, and thy gold to refine.

The soul that on Jesus hath leaned for repose,
I will not, I will not desert to his foes;
That soul, though all hell should endeavor to shake,
I'll never, no never, no never forsake.

She hadn't experienced any "fiery trials" like some people had, but her life needed plenty of refining. Was she leaning on Jesus for rest and peace? Her life was moving along pleasantly enough, so how could she tell? But, having heard people say they'd prayed for patience, and then God gave them all sorts of opportunities to practice it, she wasn't sure she wanted to pray for trials in order for her faith to be strengthened.

The students had been told no class would be held on Sunday afternoon, so Dani started her sketch of Moju. She drew several quick poses and then started a larger, more detailed one on a fresh sheet in the sketchpad. Keith should see this Indian. Would Moju be around when the plane arrived?

During Monday's class Dani's three pupils drew people again, this time trying to show motion or action. She felt disheartened but encouraged them that practice makes perfect and they needed to continue drawing after she left. Tuesday they met outside. She let them draw what they wished, while she made suggestions on how to improve. But she felt restless, knowing Keith was on his way and should arrive any minute.

Brenda stood and stretched. "I need to go back to the house for a bit."

"I'll use sign language if I have to tell them anything while you're gone." Dani sat on the log near Moki and opened her sketchpad to draw something—anything—to occupy time. And then she heard the faint sound of an airplane.

Saika jumped up, abandoning his sketch. "The sky boat!" Dani figured he said. He headed for the airstrip.

The other two students followed. In fact, the village seemed to empty out. Ben headed for the airstrip also, but Brenda wasn't with him.

Dani longed to see Keith but didn't want to appear overly eager. He would be walking up the trail soon, probably within 20 minutes. She would use the time to add details to the drawing of Moju. In only a moment she became completely engrossed. She didn't realize people were returning until there was a commotion beside her.

Two young men were staring at the drawing. One called out to Moju, who strode over and looked down. Instantly his face became a mask of terror, then rage. He took several steps back, drawing an arrow into his bow, and pointed it straight at Dani's heart.

Someone gasped.

Eyes wide, Dani held her breath. At this range Moju would not miss his target. It happened so fast, she had no time to cry out to God for deliverance.

Keith burst into the space between her and the thunderous warrior and grabbed the arrow tip with his right hand, pushing it downward toward the ground. Unflinching, he stared into Moju's eyes. "Ben!"

Stepping forward, Ben bid Sasi to interpret.

"Ask him why he wants to harm her," Keith directed.

Ben changed the words into Yabeja. Sasi modified them so Moju could understand. Moju spat out a reply; the translation procedure was reversed.

"He says the woman captured his spirit on her white leaf, which is taboo in his tribe. To ensure his spirit is returned to him, she must either become his wife or die."

Dani gasped and instinctively rose from the log. Keith's left arm reached back in a protective motion, indicating she was to stay behind him, which she was quite willing to do.

"Tell him she belongs with me. She goes with me in the sky boat when I leave tomorrow morning." Keith's next words were in Portuguese; the only word Dani caught was the one for "wife." The conversation continued for several minutes before Keith said, without turning his head to look back, "Give me the picture, Dani."

Her hands trembled as she tore it from the sketchpad and slipped it into his left hand.

Keith held it out to Moju. "Ben, tell him he may tear it into little pieces, or burn it, or keep it. His spirit is returned to him with humble apologies. The woman did not mean to offend him. She didn't know his customs."

Sasi translated. Moju shook his head and spoke again.

"He says this isn't enough retribution," Ben replied. "What now?"

"We need to find some *jeito*. Does he want food in payment?"

The answer was no. Moju asked for Keith's watch.

Keith hesitated only an instant. "Tell him he can have it, if he puts away the arrow."

The warrior and the pilot stared at each other. Moju gave a slight nod. Keith let go of the arrow so the Indian could return it to the quiver. Keith removed his chronograph and handed it over with the picture. Moju grunted, put the watch on, and stalked into the jungle.

Brenda immediately appeared at Dani's side and, murmuring soothing words, led her back to the house. As reaction set in, Dani sank onto the nearest bench, put her head in her hands, and wept. In a few minutes Brenda handed her a cup of coffee, which she drank slowly.

"I think you should stay in the house a while," Brenda suggested, "and, although I'll miss you, it's good you're leaving in the morning."

"Do you think he'll make more trouble for me?"

"I don't trust him. He's not like the Yabeja men. He seems to reason differently and act strangely. I'll be glad when his buddy, Zio, gets well enough to leave, or when the Indian Agency decides to relocate them. I hope it happens before he decides to take a girl from our village as his wife. I've seen the way Moju looks at the young girls. I've warned their mothers to keep a close watch over them."

Dani didn't leave the house the rest of the afternoon. She helped Brenda with supper preparations, packed her clothes, and put her art supplies in plastic bags. A sense of foreboding hung over her. The flight home couldn't happen soon enough. She wanted to get out of here before anything else went wrong.

Keith. What was he thinking? She had messed up his life. He would hate the sight of her from now on. No, he'd probably keep on tolerating her just because he was a wonderful Christian. But he could have been killed. He had risked his life because of her mistake in committing Moju's likeness to paper. And he'd given up his chronograph to bail her out. She felt absolutely awful.

Dani was preoccupied and quiet at supper, reflecting and praying silently about what had happened. When she got up to clear the table with Brenda, Keith asked, "Will you walk with me to the airstrip to check on the plane?"

She shrugged. Why would he want her along?

"Go ahead," Brenda said. "I can do the dishes tonight."

When they stepped outside, Keith paused and gazed around the village. "The coast is clear. Let's go. How did your art classes go this week?"

"Fine."

"How many people did you teach?"

"Three."

"Who were they?"

"Saika, Jabuti, and Moki. Two men, one woman."

"Do they show promise?"

She sighed. He was trying to draw her out of her moodiness, but she felt beyond repair. How he could be so nice to her after what had happened, she didn't know.

KCT was parked at one edge of the airstrip. They walked a circle around it as Keith looked it over and made sure the door was still locked. "No sign of tampering," he affirmed.

"About this afternoon—" she ventured.

"We don't have to talk about it. I can tell you're still upset."

"But I haven't thanked you yet for stepping in and saving me. You acted so fast. I was petrified when he aimed that arrow at me."

"Pilots have to act quickly. Sometimes it's a reaction. I wasn't going to stand by and let him kill you."

"Then you gave him your watch. I know they're expensive. I don't know how I'll ever repay you so you can buy a new one."

"You don't need to. I'm not hurting for money. I'll replace it when we get back to the city. The important thing was your safety. Replacing *you* would be impossible."

"Sounds like what my parents said when I got lost at a Homes and Gardens show years ago. Unfortunately for you, you're stuck with me until we get back to Belém tomorrow." Something bright-colored caught her eye. She looked at the trail to the village and saw Moju. Dani gasped.

Without turning, Keith put a hand on her arm. "What's wrong?"

"Moju," she whispered. "He's at the edge of the trail."

"Alone?"

Dani nodded.

Keith took her other arm also, his hazel eyes darkening in intensity. "Listen, Dani, I told him he couldn't have you because you belong with me. Now he's watching us to see if it's true, so we're going to convince him. Make this look good." He pulled her against his chest, bent his head, and kissed her.

She lost all sense of time and space. Dani forgot to breathe and began to get light-headed.

Keith stopped to catch a breath first. He kissed the tip of her nose and then her forehead. "Is he still there?"

The question brought her back to earth with an inaudible thud. His kiss had been merely an act to fool the Indian. For one brief moment she had lost herself in possibilities that didn't exist. The disappointment was keen. "I don't see him. He's not where he was, at least. But he could be behind a tree."

He took her by the elbow and steered her to the path.

She didn't want to go. Dusk had arrived. Would Moju jump them as they walked back to the village? Could Keith sense her reluctance to walk that direction? But an alternate route through the jungle was too perilous to even consider.

Keith chatted about the flight plan for the return to Belém. Dani half paid attention. His words were probably to make Moju think they were having a normal conversation, if indeed he was following them.

When they reached the door of the house, Keith dropped his hand from her elbow and murmured, "That was good acting back there, Daniela Austin."

Her head jerked up. "Pardon me?"

"The kiss."

Without stopping to think, she retorted, "I'm an artist, not an actress." Then she turned on her heel and walked inside.

SIXTEEN

Keith had been awake half the night wondering how he should deal with the fallout from kissing her. *Just act as if nothing happened,* he told himself.

He sipped from the coffee mug Brenda had handed him and glanced at the dark circles under Dani's eyes. Had she slept at all? What had been a good village experience for Dani until yesterday, according to Ben, had gone awry. Keith needed to get her out of this place and back to the city.

Brenda had fixed eggs, biscuits, and coffee from the wealth of supplies Keith had flown in. They would sit around the table and talk for hours if he didn't make the move. Keith stood. "Thanks for the hospitality, folks, but Dani and I need to get going." He'd already been down to the plane with his gear, so he reached for Dani's bag and let her carry the art supplies.

The Tatums and many of the villagers accompanied them to the airstrip. Moki, carrying her baby in her arms, walked beside Dani. She spoke, smiled, and touched Dani's arm.

Was Dani going to cry? Keith was relieved when she smiled back at Moki. Jabuti and Saika shook Dani's hand as they'd seen Ben do. Again she smiled. She hugged Brenda, thanked both her and Ben, and turned to climb into the plane.

"Up you go." Keith offered her a hand up; she slid over his seat to the passenger seat. He climbed in and fastened her seat belt and harness, adjusting it to fit properly.

Dani looked out the window and shivered.

"Surely you're not cold."

"Moju. At the edge of the clearing." She dropped her gaze to her lap.

"We'll be on our way in just a few minutes." Keith shut the door and snapped his belt and harness. The crowd moved away from the Cessna. "In an hour and a half we'll be back in Belém."

"Ah, civilization, sweet civilization," Dani sighed. "I am not cut out for roughing it. The last week's been an adventure. It was made tolerable because of the Tatums' great hospitality, but I don't intend to repeat the experience. I cherish hot showers, electric stoves and fridges, and stores within walking distance."

He smiled and strapped on his kneeboard. He unclipped yesterday's completed flight plan and slid it underneath today's return schedule. "Well, Dani," he said lightly, "I'm going to have to depend on your watch to tell time so I can radio in my checkpoints at planned intervals."

"Oh, of course. I'm sorry." She handed it over.

He fastened the slim watch to the control yoke, where it looked so funny they both grinned. *Ah, Dani,* he thought. *I'm glad your sense of humor is returning.*

"Let's have a word of prayer," he said aloud. "Lord, thank You for this glorious new day. We ask that You grant safety, good judgment, and a smooth flight. In Jesus' matchless name, Amen."

"Amen," Dani echoed.

Through the open window, Keith yelled "Clear," and started the engine. He put KCT through the run up; it checked out fine. Full throttle was applied. The plane rolled down the bumpy, grass strip. Then they were airborne. The village of Yabewa faded away. He radioed Tammy that they were in the air.

A minute later he turned to Dani. "Sitting in the front, you can see the instruments as well as scenery."

"I haven't a clue what they all do."

"Easy to remedy." He explained what each instrument was for and was pleased she seemed fascinated.

Suddenly he felt a momentary roughness in the engine that smoothed out before he could blink. Had he only imagined it? All the instrument readings were normal. Maybe it was only a wind gust. But now he was more alert, more on edge. If he felt it again, they'd turn back and land so he could thoroughly check the engine.

After his next call-in, Dani stared out the window. "The trees look like a broccoli carpet far below us. All the fuss in the

States about the rain forests being destroyed! They need to see how many trees are still around."

"I hope that never changes. I can fly for hours and see only trees and rivers." He radioed in his second checkpoint.

Moments later they heard a loud "pop." The engine started vibrating. Keith immediately checked the instruments. Within seconds he smelled gas and then smoke. Although Dani didn't speak, he sensed her alarm. Her eyes were on him, but he was busy looking at the fuel flow meter. He turned off the fuel tank selector, preventing more gas from feeding the fire, and radioed, "Mayday!" He gave time and heading. The smoke smell was stronger. He turned off the master switch and pushed the nose down. "Hang on, Dani. We're going down."

"Lord, help us," she prayed.

They were going down fast. No airstrip, field, or river was close enough for an emergency landing. What chance did they have of surviving a crash into trees?

Lord, we are Yours. If this is our time, then it's OK. But I pray You'll spare us.

He leveled out the Cessna, gliding above the treetops. A tree taller than the others clipped the right wing tip, flipping the plane nose down between several trees. A jarring thud, then darkness.

"Dani! Dani!"

The voice sounded far away. She couldn't respond.

Fingers pressed against her neck, feeling for a pulse. Why didn't they go away and let her sleep? The hands belonging to the fingers shook her shoulders. She felt pain.

"Dani, wake up! We've got to get out of here. You've got to help me!"

Keith. The voice belonged to Keith. Dani fought her way out of the darkness and opened her eyes slowly. Concerned hazel eyes stared at her.

"Thank God," he murmured.

She hung against the shoulder harness. "It hurts to breathe."

"You may have some broken ribs. Brace your arms against my shoulders while I unharness you." A bloody gash adorned

Keith's forehead, another his arm. As he took off her harness, she sagged against his chest. He held her for a moment and whispered against her hair, "I've got to get you out of here, which won't be easy. You have to be brave."

Dani looked down, astounded that the instrument panel was so close to her legs. Splashes of blood were on both sides of the panel. So she was bleeding, too?

"Can you move your legs?"

She wiggled her feet. "I think so."

"Thank You, God." Keith began to tug and maneuver her across the cabin toward the door. "The engine smashed through the fire wall and pushed the instrument panel at us. Amazing our legs weren't crushed or broken."

What a nauseating thought. She fought down the bile.

He had her out of the wreckage now. "Sit by this tree, Dani. I'm going back in for the survival kit and machete."

Looking at KCT, Dani didn't know how they'd survived, and with no serious injuries. The Cessna had clipped several trees as it descended, resting nose down at more than a 90-degree angle. Vines were tangled about the fuselage and wings. Both wings were bent back but were still attached, with gaping holes in them, as well as in the cargo pod. The tail section bent upward from the fuselage. Fuel dripped from the wing tanks. Was there a chance of fire even now? And Keith was inside the plane climbing around! What if those vines didn't hold the plane, and it toppled over with him inside?

She took a deep breath. Pain stabbed her rib cage. Shallow breaths were better. *Please, Lord, keep him safe in there.*

The plane swayed slightly as Keith moved over the seats, but the vines held tight. At last he moved to the cargo door, which stood ajar, and dropped the two-foot-by-two-foot metal survival kit onto the ground, and then the machete. He jumped down, picked them up, and walked to her.

Thank You, Jesus. She felt weak with relief.

From the first-aid kit Keith produced hydrogen peroxide and cleansed the wounds on her legs. Next he dabbed the solution on his arm and forehead. He bandaged her deeper cuts and put Mercurochrome on the others.

Dani bandaged his arm. "The gash on your forehead is rather deep. You probably should have stitches, but I guess that's impossible right now."

"Do you know how to make a butterfly bandage?"

"No."

"If we had a mirror, I'd put it on myself. You'll have to help me out." He fashioned the butterfly from adhesive tape and told her how to apply it.

Her fingers trembled. His nearness was disquieting. The last time they'd been this close . . .

Keith stepped away and pulled an ugly, army-green can from the survival kit. "Guess what's in here?" He shook the large can, and she shook her head. "Water. Are you thirsty."

"Very."

He punched the can open with his Swiss army knife. "Drink sparingly. We've got to make these four cans last until we can find a river or else get rescued."

Dani took several swallows and passed it back. After he drank, he carefully set the can down and covered the top with an extra piece of gauze.

"Now we need to pray." Keith reached over and took one of her hands in his. "Lord, we prayed for safety, but You chose to allow this. We don't understand, but we accept Your sovereignty. Thank You for sparing us from the engine fire and the crash. We believe You want us alive for a reason, so we ask You to send rescuers soon. Protect us from the jungle dangers. Help us know what to do to increase our chance of survival. Give us Your peace in this 'storm.' In Jesus' name, Amen."

Dani inhaled deeply and winced in pain.

Keith noticed. "I wish I could get you to a doctor." He sighed. "If your ribs are broken, I could wrap tape around you."

She blushed. "No, thank you; I'll wait. I need to remember to not breathe deeply. And please don't say anything funny to make me laugh." She looked at the wreckage. "What now?"

"The first thing is to get you into clothes that will give you more protection from bugs. At least you're wearing tennis shoes rather than sandals. Do you have a long-sleeved shirt and slacks in your suitcase?"

"Neither. All I brought was culottes and tank tops, just like these. And everything is still in the plane."

"I'll get our stuff."

"Keith!"

"I'll be careful, I promise." He walked back to KCT and extracted from the pod his gear, her suitcase, and her art supplies, which they'd forgotten in all the excitement. He handed her a shirt and a pair of pants. "These are my extras. Put them on."

"I'll be swimming in them." She began pulling the clothes on over her own.

"I think we can remedy that some." From a rope in his gear, he cut a belt and two short lengths to tie around the rolled-up pant cuffs. "You won't win a beauty contest in these, but they'll do the job."

She rolled the sleeve cuffs several times until they met her wrists. She was trying not to give in to panic, but the emotions were beginning to swamp her. "How will anyone find us?"

"Tammy was flight-following, remember? I had just radioed in a checkpoint two minutes before I called 'Mayday,' so she knows the general area we're in. By now she's reported to Roy, and he's phoned S.E.R.A.C. and probably Bentes. Planes will be sent to search this area."

She looked up at the canopy of trees and shivered. "How will they be able to see us?"

"KCT is equipped with an E.L.T.—emergency locator transmitter—in the empennage, which self-activated when we crashed."

"The empennage?"

"The tail cone. The E.L.T. turns itself on at impact, sending out a radio signal, which can be picked up by rescue planes when they fly nearby. They can pinpoint our exact location with it—as long as we stay with the plane and don't try hiking out."

"How will they land to get us?"

"They'll have to land at the nearest airstrip and hike in. In the meantime, we've got work to do here. I'm pretty sure we're not going anywhere today."

"A night out here in the jungle?"

Keith touched her arm reassuringly. "Pretend we're at camp. We're roughing it for a day and night."

Dani glanced at the enormous trees, the lush foliage, and undergrowth. "My idea of a campground features mowed lawns between well-spaced trees, bathroom facilities, and a warm shower. Have you done this kind of camping before?"

"I had survival training. And, I must say, I enjoyed it." He took the machete and began clearing the area around the nearest tree.

"Great. Because I know absolutely nothing. I'm a hundred-percent city girl. I bet snakes live out here."

"Yes. Just stay where you are. You'll be all right."

She felt totally useless and helpless. She sat and watched him work, the bandage on his arm turning red as the wound bled again from the exertion. But he refused to stop until a wide path to the next large tree was cleared. Then he took a break. She changed the bandage for him.

"I'm starved. Let's picnic," he said as she finished.

"Sure. Just let me spread the red-and-white tablecloth."

"Oh, you found it in the picnic hamper?" When she frowned at him, he added gently, "The survival kit does contain food."

Dani's stomach rumbled. "Like what?"

"Granola." She rolled her eyes, but he continued, "High in protein—good for energy."

"What time is it? Oh. Neither of us has a watch now."

"I found the remains of yours near the instrument panel. But I'd guess it's 1 o'clock. We'll have to tell time by our inner clocks, since we can't see the angle of the sun."

They ate some granola and sipped more canned water.

"Why did the plane catch fire?" Dani asked.

"Until we get the engine inspected, we won't know for sure, but I think the 'pop' we heard was a cylinder breaking. The smell of gas meant the fuel injector line broke, allowing fuel to spray over the hot engine. The fuel ignited. We smelled smoke. I put the plane into the quick descent in an attempt to blow out the fire, but even so, we were committed to land immediately.

Unfortunately we had no airstrip, field, or river from which to choose."

"Was the engine old?"

"Age shouldn't have been a factor. The time on it was well within the limits set by the F.A.A. But sometimes—rare as it may be—a factory rebuilt engine has a faulty cylinder that breaks."

"What if Moju did something—"

"No. The pre-flight check showed nothing amiss." He ran a hand through his hair. "By now Roy will have notified our mission headquarters. The safety officer will be sent to do an investigation. He'll have to ask you questions, too."

"Like what?"

"What you observed. Did I to try to prevent the accident? How did I act and react? He has to rule out pilot error—that I was at fault."

"Well, I'll set him straight."

Keith rewarded her with a wide grin that showed his dimple. "Thanks, Dani. And now I'd better clear more jungle so I can rig up the hammocks while we still have enough daylight."

"I don't have a hammock."

"I keep an old army jungle hammock in the pod for emergency use. I haven't checked it for a few months, but it should be in good repair."

"Anything I can do to help?"

"Why don't you sketch KCT for me?"

"Like that?"

Keith looked over at the wreckage. "Yeah, like that. We don't have a camera. Showing how it looks today might be important for the investigation."

Dani set to work, the paper feeling damper than usual. Keith had to do all the physically demanding work while she just drew. She sketched KCT from several angles. Was this really helpful, or was he merely keeping her occupied?

In another hour Keith finished clearing a large area around three sturdy trees he could use for hammock posts. He sat down and wiped his dripping forehead with his sleeve. The bandages were again stained red. "You can change them later, when we're done setting up." He sighed. "I need to rest a bit before hanging the hammocks." He leaned back against the tree and closed his eyes.

Dani studied his face but squelched the urge to reach out and touch him, to smooth the lines in his forehead. He was having to bear the burden of the crash. Her being here only added to his work and responsibility.

They sat quietly for minutes. Dani began to notice jungle noises—birds, cicadas, and little rustlings—she hadn't heard while he was chopping and slashing brush.

He opened his eyes. "Would you like to help me put up the hammocks?"

"If I can." She set aside the sketchpad.

"You hold up one end here while I string the other end to that tree," he instructed. Soon Keith's Brazilian hammock, with its own mosquito net, hung between the two large trees. He picked up one end of the old jungle hammock, and Dani grabbed the other. As he strung one side to one of the trees to which his hammock was attached, she backed toward the third tree and stretched out the army-green hammock.

She heard a whisper of movement in the underbrush of the uncleared jungle near her shoe. She dropped the hammock as if it were a hot potato and screamed.

"Don't move!" He grabbed the machete and raced to her side, slashing downward with the tool in several short arcs.

Dani forgot about being brave or helpful. She forgot her ribs hurt whenever she took more than just a shallow breath. Maybe reaction from the crash had finally set in. She screamed again, and then a third time.

Keith dropped the machete and took her by the arms. "Did it bite you? Calm down, Dani! Tell me if it bit you!"

She trembled from head to toe, still screaming.

He knelt, untied the ropes around the cuffs, pulled up the pant legs, and examined her skin. Not finding any fang marks, he stood and gently shook her. "Stop it, Dani. You're all right now. The snake is dead."

"I hate snakes!" she yelled in mounting hysteria. "I hate the jungle! Get me out of here!"

Keith pulled her into his arms, holding her tight while she tried to struggle. Over and over he repeated, "We're going to be all right, Dani. We're going to get out of this alive."

Finally she ceased fighting his hold and relaxed against his chest.

"That's it, Sweetheart," he said.

The words didn't register in her benumbed brain until hours later.

SEVENTEEN

Just before dusk Keith climbed into KCT to turn off the E.L.T. in order to save the batteries. But he'd have to climb back in to re-activate it in the morning.

"No one flew over," Dani grumbled. "Not one plane."

"Someone will fly over us and pick up the signal. It's just a matter of time. The most important factor is that God knows where we are."

She sighed audibly. "I know that in my head, but the rest of me isn't cooperating yet."

He squeezed her shoulder reassuringly. "Time to try out the hammocks before the mosquitoes find us. In you go; I'll zip it up for you." He held it steady as she gingerly lay down in the narrow, hot, and uncomfortable army-surplus hammock.

"Is this equipped with seasick pills?"

He chuckled. "The emergency kit isn't that extensive. But I can guarantee you won't fall out during the night. I tested the knots I tied. But, more importantly, the Bible says, 'Underneath are the everlasting arms,' so try to mentally picture it."

She wanted to be calm like him, wanted to cling to the fact that God held them in His hand. But fear and doubts assailed her.

Dani had a miserable night. In spite of the stabilizer bar, the hammock swayed whenever she shifted her weight or position. She was hungry, thirsty, and very scared of the jungle noises and the possibility they might never be found. Bloodthirsty mosquitoes buzzed in cacophony. How many carried malaria? At least the green netting offered protection from bites, if not from the sound.

How could Keith sleep through all the noise? Of course, he'd done so much work clearing the area, he was tired enough to conk out.

Dani tried silently reciting all the Bible verses she could remember about God's sovereignty, love, and peace. Yet she was more scared than she'd ever been in her 21 years. Keith was only 10 feet away. She knew he wouldn't let any jungle animals get her. Was she putting more trust in him than in God?

Lord, I want to trust You. Please help me!

She mentally relived the accident and the incident with Moju. She thought of the snake and shivered again. She hadn't needed to ask if it was poisonous; the way Keith had chopped it to pieces, she'd known it wasn't a plain, old garden variety.

In the last two days Keith had saved her life several times. She'd been such a nuisance to him. Did he wish she weren't here? If he had only himself to take care of, the ordeal would be so much easier.

"I'm sorry to be an added burden," she whispered.

The other hammock moved. "Dani?" Keith called softly. "Are you awake?"

"Yes."

"Slept any?"

"No."

"You've got to try. You'll need every ounce of energy."

She didn't want to ask him "why?" She chose another topic instead. "What did you say to Moju when you switched to speaking Portuguese? I only understood the word for 'wife.'" Suddenly it was important to know.

He didn't answer immediately. Had he fallen back asleep?

"I told him you couldn't cook over a fire, clean animal skins, or tan hides," he sheepishly confessed. "You weren't used to planting or harvesting a garden, pounding out rice, hauling water, or washing clothes in the river. So you wouldn't make him a good wife."

Chagrined, she said, "Well, that's for sure. But did you tell him I was your wife?" She was still puzzling over the kiss.

"Not exactly. I didn't actually lie to him. But through careful wording, I did let him think you were my wife so I could get you out of a very dangerous situation."

"So you think he would have killed me?"

"Let's just say his moment of hesitation after he drew back the arrow was a Godsend."

Something chattered in the treetops. She tensed. "What's that?"

"Sounds like monkeys."

"I'm scared, Keith. I've tried saying verses and praying, but I'm still very scared."

"Psalm 4:8 is a good verse to remember: 'In peace I will both lie down and sleep, for You alone, O Lord, make me to dwell in safety.' I like Psalm 32:7, too: 'You are my hiding place; You preserve me from trouble; You surround me with songs of deliverance.'"

"You memorized verses on safety."

"Don't sound so surprised. Why wouldn't I? They're good verses for anyone to know. And I know songs, too."

Keith launched into a medley of hymns and she joined him, pondering the words and beginning to relax.

Under His wings, I am safely abiding,
Though the night deepens and tempests are wild,
Still I can trust Him; I know He will keep me,
He has redeemed me, and I am His child.
Under His wings, under His wings,
Who from His love can sever?
Under His wings, my soul shall abide,
Safely abide forever.

Every joy or trial falleth from above,
Traced upon our dial by the Sun of Love;
We may trust Him fully all for us to do.
They who trust Him wholly find Him wholly true.
Stayed upon Jehovah, hearts are fully blest
Finding, as He promised, perfect peace and rest.

Though Satan should buffet, though trials should come,
Let this blest assurance control,
That Christ has regarded my helpless estate,
And hath shed His own blood for my soul.
It is well, with my soul,
It is well, it is well, with my soul.

Keith prayed aloud for Dani to sense God's peace and security and that she'd be able to sleep.

As she drifted off in the predawn hours, she thought he said again, "That's it, Sweetheart." The words once again were tucked away in her memory to ponder later.

Jungle sounds awakened her. Light filtered through the foliage. She wondered what time it was. She stood and stretched her stiff muscles but sucked in her breath at the pain in her ribs.

"Good morning, sleepy head."

How could he smile? She groaned.

"Ready for some grub?"

Her stomach rumbled. "More of the same, I take it."

"Yes, milady. Delectable emergency rations."

Missing her morning coffee, Dani's head ached. She was determined, though, to be pleasant and not her usual grumpy self when she didn't have enough caffeine in her system. At least they had something to eat and drink. She was thankful for that small blessing.

After a breakfast of granola and water, Keith reactivated the E.L.T. Then he cleared a path into the jungle as he searched for vines containing water.

Dani took her Bible from her baggage. The thin pages felt limp from the humidity. She turned to various Psalms to focus her thoughts on God and His sustaining power and grace.

Psalm 94:17-19 was especially meaningful. "If the Lord had not been my help, my soul would soon have dwelt in the abode of silence. If I should say, 'My foot has slipped,' Your lovingkindness, O Lord, will hold me up. When my anxious thoughts multiply within me, Your consolations delight my soul."

She could picture anxious thoughts multiplying like jungle mosquitoes. She spent some time praying God would deal with her anxiety and console her with His love and presence.

Then she sketched the hammocks and trees as she considered Keith's words: "That's it, Sweetheart." She was now sure he had said them twice. Did the words mean what she thought, what she hoped, or was he just saying them to calm her down—a verbal pacifier?

For months she'd tried to accept a little sister/big brother relationship with Keith Kelcey. She had told herself wishing for more interest on his part was futile. She couldn't compete with Maggie's poise and beauty. She was just a kid with no hope of gaining Keith's heart.

Had the incident with Moju and the accident caused a shift in their relationship? Why had Keith used the word "sweetheart" not once, but twice? A mere slip of the tongue? Or dared she hope he knew what he'd said? And not only knew, but meant it?

"Dani!" He strode into view holding a long vine. "Grab those two empty cans, please."

She did. He poured liquid from the vine into them.

"I also found another one. I'll show you." He took one of her hands and led her down the path he'd made.

She stepped gingerly and hoped no snakes were around. Keith cut the vine, upended it, laughingly poured some down her throat, and drank what was left.

"I do believe you're enjoying yourself."

"Why not?" His hazel eyes twinkled. "As they say, no use crying over spilt milk or wrecked Cessnas"

"How will you get another plane to fly?"

"In time the mission will replace KCT. Someone higher up will choose which particular plane to buy. Then our Stateside mechanics will check it over completely and make the necessary modifications for jungle flying, which could take six to eight months. I guess I should take a short furlough while they're working everything out. In the meantime, whenever a flight is required by one of our Belém teams, a pilot from one of our other centers will have to fly a plane to the area."

Furlough? Dani's heart sank. Keith would leave, and she'd be in Belém sketching. By the time he returned, she'd be gone.

Suddenly he straightened, turning his head toward the north. "Listen!"

She heard nothing.

"A plane's approaching. Let's get back to the 'camp.'"

For the next hour Keith paced as the plane flew a search pattern in the area. Every so often he lifted his arms and said,

"Lord, send them over here. We're over here. Please let them fly this way and find the signal." At last the plane began to circle overhead. "You've got it!" he yelled. "Thank you, God!"

But then the plane's drone grew fainter.

"What's happening?" Dani grabbed his unhurt forearm. "Why are they leaving?"

He laid a hand over hers. "They can't land here, remember? They've got to find the nearest strip and then hike in. Believe me, they know we're in here."

"How can you be so sure?"

"It's my vocation, not my hobby." Months ago she had said those words. Keith picked her up and whirled her around.

"Stop! My side! Keith, please stop!"

"I'm sorry!" He set her down.

They both dissolved in giggles in an emotional reaction to the plane finding them. They walked back to the log, sitting down to wait and to thank God for an imminent rescue.

Dani expected to be out of there by lunchtime. They weren't. Keith had grown quieter in the intervening hours. And he didn't want any food.

"Surely we don't need to ration it now," she said. "You're not refusing the granola because you know something I don't know, are you?"

He shook his head.

"We are going to be out of here today, aren't we?"

He rubbed one hand through his auburn hair. His face looked suddenly pale, his eyes shadowed with pain.

"What's wrong?"

"My head hurts. I need to lie down for a while." He stood and headed toward his hammock.

She intercepted him. "Let me see your wounds. While I don't know much about nursing, I do know redness around the wounds means infection."

He crawled into the hammock, but not before she saw that the skin around the bandages wasn't red. "Let me sleep," he said. "But if you hear a plane, wake me up."

"Sure, Keith."

She kept a silent vigil the next two hours. At one point the hammock was shaking, but she thought Keith was merely restless. She didn't put together the clues. And then she heard an aircraft approaching.

"Keith!" She hurried to his hammock. "Wake up! I think a helicopter is almost here." The only reply was a moan. She shook the hammock slightly. "Keith!"

"Can't."

"Can't what?" No answer. Alarmed, she found the opening in the net and reached in to touch his terribly hot forehead. She drew her hand back as if she'd been burned. "You can't get sick!" She grabbed his shoulder and shook him. "You can't get sick," she repeated in desperation. "I don't know what to do."

She looked frantically around the site as if she'd find an answer there. Keith had done all the work; he had the survival knowledge. She was totally dependent upon him. And now, if the helicopter couldn't land or help them . . . "You've got to tell me what to do!"

"Thirsty."

She brought a can and tried to lift him up with one arm so he could drink. The task wasn't easy, but she finally managed to get water down his throat.

"Love you."

The words were so soft, she almost didn't hear them as she let him sink back down. "Boy, are you delirious. I'm not Maggie."

"Dani, love you," he uttered. And then he fell asleep again.

Her shaking fingers brushed his cheek and felt the sandpaper roughness of a 32-hour beard. If only he meant the last sentence.

Keith didn't move a muscle. She looked at the treetops and finally caught a glimpse of the chopper. Was it Bentes? How could she get his attention?

The helicopter hovered above the space where KCT had clipped several trees. A package was dropped out and fell to the jungle floor. Dani ran to it, forgetting about possible snakes. She tore it open, finding a compact two-way radio amidst sacks of food and medical supplies.

She ran back to Keith and shook him again. "You've got to tell me how to use this radio!"

He struggled to push himself up onto one elbow and stared at the device in her hand.

The vacant look in his eyes frightened her but also goaded her adrenaline to kick in again. "I'm depending on you, Keith. You can't let me down. Tell me how to turn this on and talk to Bentes."

That seemed to penetrate the fog he was in. Taking the radio from her, he fumbled with the switch and turned it on. "Kelcey to chopper." He lay back exhausted.

She heard Portuguese words over the airwaves, but understood only the word "Kiko." She reclaimed the radio and pushed the switch as he had done. "Kiko!" Her voice caught; she almost wept. "Help us. Keith is very sick. I don't know what to do!"

"Men are on their way to you through the jungle, Daniela," he said in his accented English, "but will not make it there today. Do you have major injuries?"

"No, thank God. Just cuts and maybe broken ribs. But now Keith is burning up with fever and acts delirious."

"Probably malaria. He's had it before. The package contains water; get him to drink it. Also medicine, which should be labeled 'Aralen.' That's all you can do until the men arrive. I'm so glad you're both alive. Tomorrow I'll bring the chopper back to help pinpoint your location for the rescue team."

The whup-whup-whup of the helicopter faded. Dani switched off the radio and sobbed. Another night in the jungle? With Keith so ill?

She cried a long time. Drained of emotion, she retrieved the package and carried it to the "camp."

EIGHTEEN

The humidity was oppressive. A storm must be approaching. The jungle hammock was water-resistant, but Keith's wasn't. Dani decided to move him so he wouldn't get soaked, which was the last thing he needed with such a high fever.

She pulled aside the mosquito net and tugged his arm. "Keith, you need to change hammocks," she coaxed.

"No," he mumbled.

"You've got to help me. Please!"

He was 190 pounds of muscle. Unless he cooperated, she could not move him to the other hammock. She continued to tug on his arm. He didn't budge.

"Water."

"I'll give you some water when you're in the other hammock. Please. Try to get up." She had scanned the complex Portuguese instructions in the Aralen box and knew she had to give him one of those pills with the water he requested. Not understanding all the directions, she prayed she didn't give him the wrong dose. Too little medicine would be of no help, and too much—the thought petrified her.

"Love Dani."

She blinked back more tears, wishing with all her heart he meant those words. With sudden inspiration, she cupped his hot cheeks with her hands. "I don't believe you. If you do love me, then try to get up."

Dazed hazel eyes searched for her face. Recognition flared. He started to push himself up. Capitalizing on the momentum, she grabbed his arms and pulled. Finally he stood, leaning on her shoulders. She swayed from his weight but braced her feet and gritted her teeth.

Hearing the rain marching through the trees, getting nearer and nearer, she slid one arm around Keith's waist, ignoring the pain in her ribs. His medical need was more critical than hers.

"Walk with me. That's it. Just a bit farther." Step by halting step, they covered the short distance that seemed much farther than it actually was. She was sweating from the effort and the extra heat radiating from his body. How high was his fever?

At last Keith lay in the jungle hammock. She helped him sip water and made him take one Aralen. She zipped the hammock closed as rain began pelting down. She grabbed several plastic sheets from the package dropped by Kiko, carefully got into the other hammock, and spread them over herself. She still got wet. Was Keith keeping dry, or did that hammock leak?

The rain lasted until dusk. She checked on Keith and gave him more water. His clothes were drier than hers but not by much. In what she guessed to be two hours, the temperature had dropped about 15 degrees. She wished for a light blanket to put over him. She wished she had more medical knowledge. She wished she could understand the Portuguese instruction pamphlet inside the Aralen box. But wishing didn't make any of them happen.

"Dani." He reached for her hand; she laid it in his. His skin wasn't as hot as it had been. "What happened?"

"You got sick. Kiko said it's probably malaria."

"Kiko? Where is he?"

"Bentes's helicopter was hovering above us. Do you remember?"

His forehead furrowed in concentration. "Vaguely."

"Kiko was the pilot. He dropped a package that contained a two-way radio. I made you talk so I could see how to use it. Then I spoke with Kiko. He said men will rescue us over land. He'll be back tomorrow to pinpoint our location for them."

"Why am I in this hammock?"

His mind was definitely clearer. "Because it rained, and I knew yours wasn't water-resistant. Don't you remember walking over here?"

. "Seems more like a dream. Did I . . . say . . . anything?" His eyes, no longer vacant-looking, probed hers.

She blushed and looked away.

"Dani."

She reluctantly met his gaze. He remembered what he'd said. She could tell. "You were delirious, Keith. Don't worry; I know you didn't mean it. Here, drink more water."

He drank half the can, sloshing some onto his already damp shirt, and wiping his mouth with the back of his hand. "What if I did mean it?"

How she wished he did! But for him to pick her over Maggie was inconceivable. She swallowed the lump in her throat and said resolutely, "Then you're still delirious." Was that a flicker of pain or regret in his hazel eyes?

He sighed. "You'd better get back in the net before the mosquitoes get you. Having malaria is no fun, believe me." He started to sit up.

She pushed his shoulders down. "Stay here. I'll use your hammock."

"Are you sure?"

"Yes. One mosquito net is as good as the other. I'll tell you in the morning which 'bed' is more comfortable," she joked.

"Before you go, hand me the box of Aralen and leave a water container under my hammock. If I wake in the night, I'll take another pill."

"Another one? I don't want you overdosing. I tried figuring out the dose on the instructions, but they were written in Portuguese."

"I've been through this before, Dani. The first 24 hours you have to attack it, then ease back."

She handed him the box. His fingers tightened around hers. "Thanks, Dani. I'm sorry—"

"I know you didn't chose to get malaria," she interrupted. "Just get well quick, OK?" She pulled her hand away and moved toward the other hammock.

"I'd say 'good night', but you'd probably laugh."

"I appreciate the thought. We can always hope . . .."

If the first night was miserable, the second was worse and seemed to be interminable. Mosquitoes buzzed annoyingly around the net until she thought she might scream.

Dani was cold, wet, tired, and still scared. She had been so concerned for Keith, she'd forgotten to eat or drink anything for hours. When a tree fell perhaps 40 yards away, she cried out in fear and then felt silly. But what if a nearby tree toppled down on them? No, God had not spared them from the crash just to let that happen. Couldn't she trust Him, too, for their complete deliverance from this ordeal?

She sang softly to herself the same hymns they'd sung last night and a few more that she remembered. Then she fell into an exhausted sleep, only to be awakened by a weird laughing sound. She pressed both hands to her mouth to keep from screaming. She wanted to call out to Keith *What's that?* but didn't want to wake him. She finally slept for a few hours.

When she awoke, her stomach felt as if it had been turned inside out. Her muscles were stiff again, her body caffeine-deprived. But first things first. She got out of the hammock and found the machete. Watching for snakes, she headed for the bush behind the plane. When she returned, Keith was getting up.

"How are you feeling?" she asked.

He combed his hair with his fingers. "Other than starving? I don't suppose the package Kiko dropped contained food?"

"Only canned goods but no can opener."

"And you didn't want to pick my pocket for this?" He pulled the Swiss army knife from his jeans pocket.

Feeling foolish, she shrugged and then blushed. "I forgot. But no, I probably wouldn't have taken it from you."

"Bring on the feast, woman. We won't bother with a fire to heat up anything, since I doubt any dry wood is around."

"Not after yesterday's downpour. How nice you've got your appetite back, Sir Kelcey."

"What are our menu choices?"

She showed him all the cans. He opened three containing stew, which they devoured cold. Keith took another Aralen.

"When do you think the men will arrive?" Dani asked.

"A few more hours, at least."

She groaned and started pacing in the tiny space of the clearing.

"Dani, you're going to make me seasick now."

"With no body of water," she grumped, "and no swaying hammocks." She stopped in front of him and touched the bandage on his head. "No streaks of red. And you don't feel hot any more."

"I have felt better in my life, though, Nurse Austin. Then again, I may feel worse later. Malaria is cyclical in nature."

Fear clutched her. "What does that mean?"

"The chills and fever could return later today, tomorrow, or the next day. Or I may be lucky enough that the Aralen breaks the cycle. We'll just have to wait and see."

"Oh, wonderful. I'm just thrilled." She bit her lower lip. "I heard a laughing noise in the night."

"A bird. Did it scare you?"

She nodded. "The night was very, very long."

"You didn't get much sleep again, I take it."

"Neither hammock gets an award for comfort. I don't see why Kristy likes sleeping in one."

"She and thousands of Brazilians. You get used to it after a while."

"I don't intend to give it a while. My own pillow and soft bed with sheets are beckoning."

"First we have to get out of here. For your sake, Dani, I hope it happens today."

Her breath caught and her eyes widened. "What?"

He hesitated. "You need to realize our rescue could take a bit longer. Do you have a comb?"

"Sure. I'll go get it for you."

"Not for me. For you."

Her hands smoothed her unruly curly hair, which she hadn't thought of combing for the last 24 hours. Anger rose within. She snapped, "I'm sorry I look awful! What do you expect out here—a beauty shop? Miss America? The Maggie Paige look? How would she look after two days of wearing baggy men's clothes in the middle of the jungle?"

"Stop it," he warned in a low voice. "I'm not comparing you to Maggie, so simmer down. I think you're cute, even when your hair is messed up. I figured you'd want to comb it before the men get here. I thought it might make you feel better."

Dani stomped off to her belongings and vigorously brushed her hair. Tired of being dirty and damp, she longed for a warm shower, a change of clothes, her bed and pillow—no matter how limp the sheets felt. Yet, if the rescue team didn't arrive for several more hours, would they have to spend another night in the jungle before they could hike out? She squelched the sob rising in her throat.

"Lord, I can't take much more of this," she prayed softly. "I am already on overload. Please get us out of here. Thank You that Keith seems better. I don't want him to have a relapse."

They were dangerously low on water. They both were so very thirsty. Dani volunteered to go looking close by for a vine.

"No, I'll do it." Keith got up. "Cutting them is tricky. If you misjudged your swing, you'd end up with a nasty machete cut that would require stitches. The survival kit contains a suture kit, but I don't think you'd enjoy my sewing you up."

Inwardly chafing that he refused to let her get the water, she watched as he found a vine and slashed it down. They filled two cans and had a good drink before the vine was empty.

Dani carried the cans back to camp. "I could have done it. You treat me like a kid. You're too protective of me."

A stormy look replaced the calm in his eyes. "Get used to it," he said gruffly. "I intend to be doing it for a long time."

Hands on her hips, she demanded, "And just what do you mean by that?" If she stayed in this jungle much longer, she'd lose her sanity as well as the geniality she was having difficulty dredging up as the hours passed.

A faint metallic sound in the distance precluded his reply. Keith swiveled toward the north. "I hear them! They're blazing a trail to us."

Waiting for the rescuers was terribly difficult. Keith wanted to chop more trail from their end. Dani begged him not to. She was afraid he wasn't strong enough yet. His words about malaria being cyclical scared her. But he insisted on cutting another 25 yards northward. He stopped occasionally to listen to the noises.

About noon they heard the helicopter. Keith sent her back to "camp" for the radio. When she returned with it, he was leaning against a tree and shivering.

He reached for the radio. "Will you bring me more Aralen?"

She ran back and grabbed the water and Aralen for him. If only he'd listened to reason and rested instead of working, maybe this new malaria attack could have been avoided. How bad would this one be? She could feel her nerves unraveling further from the strain and uncertainty.

Keith was talking with Kiko in Portuguese but stopped to take the medicine from her shaking hand. Another voice sounded over the radio.

"The rescue team is clearing a suitable spot nearby so the helicopter can land," Keith translated. He shivered violently. "Then they'll blaze a trail to us."

Dani took the radio from his hands and pressed the button. "Kiko, tell them to hurry. Keith's not doing well again. Another malaria attack is hitting him."

"S . . . s . . . sorry."

Although she was tempted, she would not yell at or berate him for foolishly overexerting himself and getting sick again. Casting blame was pointless now.

She helped him back to the hammock; he sank into it. Then she sat by the tree and waited for the men to arrive.

NINETEEN

Dani stared in horror as flames shot from the engine. The plane was going down fast. She struggled against the seat belt and shoulder harness. They had to get out before they fried. Moju, arrow drawn in his bow, rose from the flames and leered at her. He was going to kill her this time.

"Keith!" she screamed, only the word wouldn't escape her paralyzed throat. She tried again.

A cool hand restrained her. "Dani, wake up. You're all right. Take it easy."

Who was that? Where was Keith? Heart pounding, she forced her eyes open and squinted against the light. She was in a hospital bed, and dawn was breaking through the window.

Louise Addison patted her hand. "That's better. You were thrashing about, having a nightmare. You murmured Keith's name."

Her mouth was parched. She croaked, "Where—"

"You're in the Belém hospital."

Dani shook her head and tried again. "Keith?"

"He's down the hall in another room. Roy Davis stayed with him all night. Doctor Farias insisted you both be kept for observation. I guess you don't remember much of last night. Here, have a sip of water. Slowly, dear."

Dani sank back against the pillow. Why was her mind so foggy?

"You'll probably be released in a little while, once Doctor Farias checks you again. But he said Keith would most likely need to stay another night, so they can be sure they've got the malaria under control and his cuts aren't showing any infection. Jim will be bringing a vehicle for us to go home in, but he'll take Roy's place staying with Keith for the daytime hours. Here, let's get another sip of water down you."

"So groggy," Dani managed to say.

"Must be the sedative still wearing off. The helicopter pilot told Roy you cried for an hour. I guess you were still rather emotional in the emergency room. Doc wanted you to get a good night's rest."

Dani took a deeper breath. Something was wrapped about her middle. Her fingers searched for and met some tape.

"Doc taped you. You have four cracked ribs."

Her mind was clearing slowly. Yes, she'd gone to pieces during the rescue and wept hysterically. Somehow she'd walked to the waiting helicopter while two men carried Keith's stretcher. The safety officer, Tyler Morgan, and three Brazilians had stayed behind at the crash sight for the night so Tyler could inspect the wreckage this morning and could make arrangements to have the dismantled plane and the engine brought out to Belém.

What had Doctor Farias asked her in hesitant English? Had anyone on the rescue team mistreated her? Had Keith? As if he couldn't fathom that her city-girl nerves were frazzled from a plane crash and a three-day, two-night stay in a jungle spook house, all on top of a rather emotionally draining encounter with an Indian man who wanted to kill her over a sketch.

"I want to see Keith."

Again Louise patted her hand. "I'm sure he's asleep. I can understand you want to reassure yourself that he's OK. I imagine you're a little . . . attached to him right now, after what you've been through together."

Her words had an undercurrent. Dani frowned as she tried to pin it down.

"I mean, with only the two of you out there alone for three days and two nights, you undoubtedly formed a bond. Brother-sister, you know." Louise's eyes searched hers, as if for denial or confirmation.

Just what was she getting at? A hazy memory of Kiko also asking something strange about Keith as he helped her into the helicopter teased her mind. But what had he said? Dani sighed. "I'm so tired."

"Then rest until the doctor arrives. I'll sit here and read my Bible."

Two hours later Dani stood in her own kitchen. Home, sweet home. Her eyes misted. She choked back more tears. "Thanks for everything, Roy and Louise."

"Do you want someone to stay with you?"

She shook her head. "I'm fine. Just so thankful to see this place again. Tape or no tape on my ribs, I'm going to shower off the jungle grime and then rest."

"Plan to take it easy the next few days," Roy said. "I'll pass word around the center for folks to limit their visits. Otherwise, you'll be inundated with guests checking up on you and wanting to hear all about your adventure. Irene and I will expect you for supper tonight, though. Six o'clock."

His words about guests were more prophetic than Dani realized. The adults might have held back, but the kids didn't. And they were less hesitant to voice their questions.

"What was it like to crash?"

"How did you feel?"

"What did you eat?"

"Where did you sleep?"

"What animals did you see?"

"What did you two do to kill time?"

"Did Kelcey kiss you?" Mary Davis asked, with Kristy by her side, after some high-schoolers had left.

Whoa. Dani could feel the blush. He hadn't kissed her after the crash, but he had the night before. "Why would you think that?"

"Well, you were out there alone together."

"For a couple of days," Kristy added.

"And I overheard Miss Ruth tell Miss Maggie that she bet Keith liked you now instead of her and maybe he'd have to marry you," Mary finished.

Dani rubbed her aching head. "I'm really tired, girls."

"Oh, sorry." Kristy bounded to the door. "Maybe you should put a 'sleeping' sign out so no one bothers you. See you later."

"Good suggestion."

Dani taped the sign on the outside of the door, locked it, and closed her curtains. She pointed the fan at her bed and wearily sank onto the mattress. No swaying hammock. She ought to be able to relax and nap. But her mind went into overdrive. How many other people were asking the same questions?

She didn't want to remember the crash. She wanted to block it out of her memory. This morning's nightmare had seemed so real.

Dani reluctantly went to supper at the Davises' house. To her surprise, Tyler Morgan was also a guest. Mary and Tommy were excused and sent outside as soon as the meal ended, but the four adults stayed at the table.

"I apologize for the timing, Dani," the safety officer began. "I realize the recent events are painful memories, but while they're fresh in your mind, I'd like to ask you a few questions."

Her shoulders drooped. "All right."

"I've asked Roy and Irene to sit in on this discussion."

Dani nodded her consent.

"Tell me all about Wednesday morning. Think back to what you remember about the pre-flight events as well as the actual flight."

She did, but she had to backtrack and explain about the loss of Keith's chronograph to Moju. She described, in detail, the few minutes from the "pop" until the crash, including the knobs Keith had touched and what he'd said over the radio.

"Do you think Keith dealt with the situation in a professional manner?"

"Oh, yes. He was very calm." She met his gaze steadily. "I do not, for a moment, believe pilot error was a factor."

"Tell me what each of you did after the crash."

Except for relating Keith's affectionate words, Dani took him through the events up to the rescue late Friday afternoon. "I'm sorry I went to pieces when you arrived. I was so afraid we'd have to spend a third night out there."

"And Keith was in no condition by then to be of much help."

"That wasn't his fault! And he couldn't help it that I'm such a klutz at survival methods."

"No, of course not," Tyler soothed. "One more question for my report." He cleared his throat as if suddenly nervous.

"Would you say that Keith conducted himself in a . . . gentlemanly manner at all times?"

"Yes!" She looked at each person. Her eyes narrowed, but her cheeks colored. "What's going on? A couple of kids made insinuations today. Are they echoing what parents are saying or asking?"

Roy shifted uncomfortably. "Quite possibly. Dani. You have to be prepared for some people's, uh, curiosity."

"Morbid curiosity," she huffed. "When I arrived in June, Kristy served as my chaperone. I understood. No one knew me then, but they do now, and that ought to make a difference. Do they think it was Shangri-La out there? A three-day paradise? Why would people think the worst about us?"

"I know they shouldn't doubt your or Keith's integrity. But people are human. I imagine some questions are going to surface. I merely want you to be aware of that," Roy reiterated.

Drained of energy, Dani leaned against the back of the chair. "Mr. Morgan, if you're finished, I'd like to leave now."

He rose. "Please, call me Tyler. I'll walk you to your place and then head down to the hospital to see Keith. Thanks for the meal, Irene and Roy. See you later."

"Yes, thank you," Dani echoed.

The engine was in flames. Dani's legs were pinned. He couldn't pull her out. What could he use to pry the metal away from her? How long did he have before the tanks exploded?

"Take it easy, buddy."

Keith awoke slowly, his heart hammering, his mouth dry.

Jim Addison sat beside the hospital bed. "You were having a nightmare."

The pilot took a deep breath and exhaled slowly. "Sorry. Did I yell?"

"No. Just mumbled. Something about fire and Dani."

"Where is she?"

"Back at the center by now. Doctor Farias released her."

"And not me?"

"Nope. You get to stay one more night in this lovely accommodation."

"Why?"

"To get your malaria under control. And to make sure that gash on your forehead leaves only a minimal scar. Doc wasn't too concerned about the other cuts."

Keith looked at the I.V. attached to his arm. With his free hand he rubbed at his stubbly chin. "I bet I look a sight."

"I've seen you look better."

"Yeah, thanks."

Someone knocked on the door. Jim went to open it.

"Maggie. Let me see if he's up to having a visitor."

Keith rolled his eyes at the words he heard before Jim turned to him. Instead of being grateful, he was annoyed the visitor was Maggie and not Dani. *Lord, help me be civil and get this over with. I was hoping a showdown wouldn't be necessary. I sure don't feel like handling this now.*

"I'll just step out for a while." Jim left the door open and walked down the hall.

Maggie's eyes widened as she perched on the chair. He must appear grisly for her to look so shocked.

"I'm sure the accident was just awful," she gushed. "But you don't have to tell me all about it right now. I assume you'll be giving a report in prayer meeting next week. All of us from A.I.S. will be sure to attend so we can hear it, too. We're so glad you're alive, even though you're hurt some. And I'm sorry that horrible malaria flared up again."

She was talking so fast, his head spun. He held up a hand to stop her.

"Maggie, I appreciate the effort you made to travel by bus or taxi to see me, but—"

"I was only too happy to. Are they feeding you well? Should I sneak in a sweet treat for you? They will let you out soon, won't they?"

"Will you listen instead of talking peripherals for a moment?" Her eyes widened again, but he plunged on. "Let's get down to the heart of why you're here."

"Because I'm concerned about you. I'm your friend."

"As long as you stop right there. You know full well I have never offered you more than friendship." He saw the flicker of pain in her eyes and wished he could soften the blow. But it was time for complete honesty. He owed it to her. He owed it to Dani. "I've hoped for months you'd be the one to stop the rumors about us so you could save face. Forgive me for not making it clearer before or for not stopping them myself. But I can't allow you to go on thinking or dreaming that our relationship will ever be more."

She sat a bit straighter, her chin lifting. "I'm well aware of your feelings."

Are you? Keith wondered. "Good. I'm sorry. I didn't want to be so blunt."

She stood. "I should go now."

"Maggie, I hope we'll continue our friendship. You have a lot of great qualities to offer a friend."

"Thank you, Keith. Get well quickly."

Her perfume lingered after she did. He probably hadn't dealt with the situation well at all. Keith closed his eyes. He was weary, so weary.

Dani moved restlessly about her apartment. In the last 10 days she hadn't drawn anything worth looking at. Today she wouldn't even bother going to the office.

Her fellow missionaries were excited about Thanksgiving and having a day off to feast and relax. Some women were baking pies to share at the group dinner; others were thawing out turkeys in their fridges and comparing dressing recipes.

While Dani was indeed thankful to be alive and back in civilization, that was about all she could say. At her present rate of productiveness, she should just quit, pack up, and head for home. Being with her family by Christmastime held a measure of appeal. Sheltered by her parents in familiar surroundings, she was sure her horrible memories would eventually fade and her creativity would be restored.

She moved to the bathroom mirror to study her face. Too thin, too haggard. What did she expect with all the nightmares and lack of sleep?

Keith gave a cursory knock on her door and let himself in. Shocked at the intrusion, she stepped into the main room.

"I've been looking for you. I have the feeling you've been avoiding me."

If only he knew I'm avoiding everyone, she thought.

"Will you take a drive with me?"

"I don't want to go anywhere."

"Please? I haven't talked with you in days."

He stepped closer. She took a step back and ran into the table. Trapped.

He glanced at the blank page of her sketchpad on the table. "You were going to draw something at home today?"

She shrugged. "I haven't felt much inspiration lately."

"You look so tired. You're not sleeping well, are you? And you've lost weight."

"I've had some nightmares." She'd intended to sound casual but didn't pull it off.

"About the accident? I have, too."

His admission stunned her. "Do you relive it?"

He nodded. "Only not always the way it happened. Sometimes the plane bursts into flames before I get you out. Or the snake actually bites you and there's no detoxifier in the survival kit. Or the search plane never circles above. We have to chop our own way to the nearest town."

"I thought I was the only one with a vivid imagination."

"You have no monopoly on that." Keith grinned. The dimple on the right side of his mouth seemed deeper. "But right now I need to drive Tyler to the airport. I hope you'll ride with us. Then, after his flight leaves, we could have lunch together. Just you and I. Please say yes."

She shouldn't. She opened her mouth to say no, but he put an index finger over it.

"Y-E-S. Two-letter aren't words allowed."

"You don't give me any choice, then."

"I knew you're a smart woman."

Dani sat in the back seat of the *Gol* and mentally withdrew, which had become her coping technique the last 10 days. Would her mom be baking for the Thanksgiving feast for her brothers and their families? Would they decorate the Christmas tree soon?

After Keith helped Tyler check in for the international flight, they wandered around the souvenir shops. Dani thought of all the gifts she really ought to buy, especially if she was going home soon. She saw a beautiful geode bookend set, but the price was higher than what she'd seen downtown months ago. And they'd be very heavy to pack in her suitcase.

"Can we get some coffee?" Tyler asked.

"Sure." Keith led the way to the airport cafe. "I'm paying, so get whatever you'd like."

The men both picked out a pastry as well, but Dani took just coffee. Keith led them to a small table. The men began talking about a plane to replace KCT. Dani tuned out again.

"They're announcing your flight," Keith said after what seemed like only a few minutes.

They walked Tyler down to the boarding gate. He shook their hands.

"Thanks for everything, Ty," Keith said.

"Good to see you again, Keith, although I'd prefer meeting at headquarters when you're on furlough rather than being called out for an accident investigation. And, Dani, it was nice to meet you. Thanks for your cooperation. Take care, both of you."

As soon as the safety officer passed into the waiting room for the international gate, Keith glanced at his chronograph. "Too early for lunch, but I'm already hungry, even after that pastry."

"You bought a watch."

"I went to the *Cacique* yesterday. Ever been upstairs in that souvenir and gift shop?"

"No."

"The nice, expensive jewelry is upstairs in a separate room. Locked. You have to tell them you want in. Only one or two customers are allowed in at a time; I'm sure an armed guard watches from a back room."

Why was he looking at her strangely? Was her hair a mess?

He took her arm. They sauntered back through the airport. "By the way, I appreciate what you told Tyler about my flying."

"He knew everything I said was true. No pilot error was involved. I had complete confidence in you."

He stopped and turned toward her. "Had? Don't you have confidence in me now? What's happened, Dani? Did I say or do something to you while I had the malaria attacks? I don't remember everything."

Say something to me? Only that you loved me. She blinked away the moisture threatening to overflow her eyes.

"You were under so much stress. I wasn't able to help you, which I deeply regret. The nightmares—how often do you have them?"

"Every night."

"That's why you look so tired. Oh, I wish you hadn't been aboard when it happened. I'd give anything to have spared you the pain."

"The accident wasn't your fault."

"But I feel a barrier between us which wasn't there before. And it wasn't there the first two days after the crash, either. Level with me. What did I do or say? What's bothering you?"

"Don't, Keith," she whispered. "I can't take this now."

He rubbed his left hand through his hair in agitation but resumed walking. They strolled into the bright sunlight and headed down the sidewalk toward the parked car.

Keith laid one arm across Dani's shoulders. She tensed. He took her by the shoulders, making her face him. "Should I stop Tyler from getting on that jet because you still need to debrief or defuse more than you have? Something is going on in your pretty little head. It's hurting our relationship. Tell me, Sweetheart."

Her lower lip trembled. "Please stop calling me that."

"You're upset because I called you 'Sweetheart'? Why is it offensive? Or to say 'I love you'? I do remember saying that out in the jungle. I guess I was too sick to guard my words. For months I tried not to tell you too soon. But you thought I was delirious."

"W . . . weren't you?" she stammered.

"Delirious? Yes, I was—and still am. Deliriously in love with one Daniela Austin. But you think of me as a protector, a big brother, don't you? You probably think I stopped Moju from killing you because I'd do the same for any woman—as if I'm some chivalrous medieval knight?"

She nodded slightly, mesmerized by his rising emotion. He wasn't shouting, but an intensity and passion she had never heard before was in his voice.

"Do you have any idea how I felt when I walked into the clearing at the very moment he took aim at you? At the woman I love?"

She blinked. Her lips parted to speak, but he went on, "You think I'll marry Maggie someday, don't you? I know what people are saying, although I've given them no reason. Especially in the last four months. But that's the rumor."

She stiffened. Her gaze slid away from his. Rumors. She was sick and tired of them.

"Dani, I don't love Maggie. I never have. She knows that. You are the woman I love."

"But all those times—"

He put a finger on her lips to stop her words. "Think about them. Did you ever see me make the first move toward her other than the night we went out with you and Kiko, when my motive was to protect you? Maggie was the one who initiated contact and conversations. Showing up at prayer meeting, bowling, my birthday party, *Círio*—did I take her hand or put my arm around her like I did to you when we went to the zoo, or *Ver-o-Peso*, or the Hippie Fair?

"Forgive me for not stopping the rumors, but I figured they'd eventually die out or Maggie would tell people they weren't true. I wanted her to be able to save face. And . . . maybe I hoped you'd show just a little jealousy instead of always acting like I was merely a substitute big brother.

"The day you sketched KCT, you caught my attention and began capturing my heart," Keith continued. "When Kiko asked you out, I had to restrain myself from clobbering him. I didn't want him near you. And the next morning when I picked you up off your floor, I knew no one else stood a chance in my heart. How it happened so fast, I'll never understand. I begged God to help me take things slowly so I wouldn't scare you away."

"You didn't think I was just a bothersome kid you had to look after?"

He chuckled. "I'd like the privilege of looking after you the rest of my life." His gaze drifted to her lips. "In Yabewa I wasn't pretending. I'd wanted to kiss you for weeks. Moju provided the perfect excuse."

Keith's arms slid around her waist. She wrapped hers around his. And this kiss was so much better than the one in Yabewa.

A moment later, he murmured, "I bought something else besides my watch at the *Cacique* yesterday."

Keith dropped to one knee right there on the sidewalk. He took her left hand in his. The lights in his hazel eyes danced. "I have it in my pocket, waiting to adorn your finger. Will you marry me, Dani?"

"Yes, Sir Kelcey. A thousand times, yes."

He stood, pulled out the velvet-lined box, and slipped the ring—a sparkling diamond, flanked by two smaller topazes—onto her finger.

"Oh! What a magnificent ring! But it's too—"

A smattering of applause and cheering from onlookers they hadn't even noticed stopped her words. Dani crimsoned, but Keith bowed gallantly, smiled, and waved at the Brazilians, who seemed to love the drama.

"We must make some picture!" Dani said.

"You'll have to sketch it some day as a visible memory of this occasion." Then his lips claimed hers again.

EPILOGUE

(A glimpse into the future)

"Mom!"

At her daughter's slightly out-of-breath call, Dani looked up from stirring the skillet of *farofa* they would serve with rice and beans at the festival dinner. "Yes, Anna? And please pull the screen door closed tightly behind you. We don't want flies getting on all this food."

"Why can't I go with the guys? Uncle Ben is letting Chad go monkey-hunting with Sam and Alan. Just because I'm a girl doesn't mean—"

Brenda Tatum stopped measuring flour into a bowl. "I know it sounds fun, Anna, but in our village monkey-hunting is an activity for men only, which is why my husband didn't include you in the invitation."

"So why do the guys get to go? They're only teen-agers."

Brenda smiled at her missionary "niece." The Kelceys and Tatums had been so close over the years of serving in Brazil, they were like family. "My two sons and your brother, Chad, are old enough to be considered men here."

Anna snorted. "Yeah, and I could already be married and have kids like Moki's daughters, right, Mom?" She turned back to her mother.

Dani cocked her head. "And you and I are both glad you're not."

Anna was growing up fast. With her father's auburn hair and hazel eyes, she was already a beautiful young woman.

Sixteen-year-old Chad, with his dark hair and brown eyes, took after his mother. She couldn't believe in only a few short years he would head off to college in the States. Her two children were close, but when Chad had the chance to be with 17-year-old Sam Tatum and his 15-year-old brother, Alan, his sister took a back seat. Since Anna had a crush on Sam, being left behind today was especially disappointing. Dani wondered how she could mitigate the disappointment.

"Would you like to help us?"

Anna's shoulders slumped. "I guess. What do you want me to do?"

"You could get another sugar sack from the pantry and pour it into this container," Brenda directed. She added sugar to the bowl with flour and said to Dani, "Moki is pleased you're here for the New Testament dedication."

"Seeing her and her children and grandchildren is great," Dani admitted. "With one of her daughters knowing Portuguese, she can translate my words to Moki without my needing to bother you. I'm glad you invited us for the festivities."

"Will Janel be here soon?" Anna asked.

Although five years separated Anna from the oldest Tatum child, the two had gotten along well in past years. But Dani knew her daughter was apprehensive that a year of college in the States would have matured Janel too much to still be friends with a lowly 14-year-old.

"Your father should be flying her in on the next flight."

Brenda couldn't hide her excitement. "I can hardly wait to see her! And my parents."

Dani could imagine how she'd feel if one of her children had been gone nine months and was flying in on the Cessna. "Anna can help me with the food while you go meet the plane."

"Aunt Brenda, will Janel and I still have things to talk about?" Anna asked.

"Of course. One year of college doesn't change a person that much. I think I hear the plane now."

"Go," Dani directed. "We'll take care of the food."

Anna washed her hands and picked up the mixing spoon. "How many shuttle flights does Dad have today?"

"One more. He contracted Bentes and Kiko to fly in two more planeloads tomorrow with the rest of the guests for the ceremony."

"I'm glad we got here early. I liked the 'JESUS' video last night, even though I couldn't understand the words. Did you see how all the Yabeja were totally absorbed in watching it?"

"Yes." Dani turned off the burner and set the skillet to the side. "They haven't seen many videos. But I'm sure the message itself was as spellbinding as watching people move and talk on a screen."

"The kids didn't wiggle a bit but just stared at it."

"I admit I kept glancing at Moju. Brenda thinks he's close to making a commitment to Jesus Christ after all these years."

"He doesn't look like the pastel in the Admin building."

"Which is almost 20 years old, Anna. Moju has aged, of course, as well as adapted his style of dress to fit in here."

"Tell me again how Dad saved you from him."

"Honey, you've heard the story a zillion times."

"I know. But it's so cool."

Dani smiled indulgently. "Your father was—and is—my hero—my knight in shining armor." She stared into space a moment, as if she were traveling back in time. "The whole village has changed a lot in 20 years."

"Like how?"

She returned her gaze to her daughter. "Yabewa now has a school with several teachers, a health office, and a church with its own Yabeja pastor. This house has two extra bedrooms plus an office. Village homes have adobe walls and aluminum roofs. The people are healthier and happier. They're singing praises to God and memorizing Scripture. And, going back to Moju, he now dresses and behaves like the Yabeja."

"I guess he had no choice, did he?"

"Actually, he did. When his buddy, Zio, died, he could have walked back into the jungle or been sent to another Indian group by the agent. But the Yabeja decided to give him a home at the edge of the clearing. Then he married one of the teens. They've had four children. A couple of years ago his wife became a Christian and has prayed for his salvation ever since."

"Surely he knows enough Yabeja by now to understand the 'JESUS' video."

"I had the same thought. But understanding the words and understanding the spiritual meaning are two different things.

Only God can grant the latter, in His timing, not ours." Dani yawned.

Anna giggled. "You didn't sleep well in the jungle hammock last night, did you?"

"Twenty years hasn't changed that. I'm always amazed that your dad and you kids find hammocks comfortable. But I'm willing to put up with the pain so both Brenda's and Ben's parents and Roy and Irene Davis can have the extra bedrooms here."

"What a sacrifice," Anna teased.

"Nothing so noble. Merely a concession to those who are older. I'm done with the *farofa*, so I'll take over your task. You can go say hi to Janel. Just don't be too disappointed if she needs a little time with her parents today before she can focus on you. OK? She hasn't seen them for nine months."

"Sure, Mom. I understand. Maybe Moki needs my help watching her grandkids while she pounds rice for the big meal."

"How sweet of you to think of that."

Dani stared at the door a few moments after Anna left. Yes, her younger child was definitely growing up.

Dani wiped away tears of joy as she watched Ben Tatum hand just-off-the-press New Testaments to those Yabeja Indians who had served as co-translators over the last 20 years. Two of her art pupils, Jabuti and Saika, were among the group of five men.

Keith gave her hand a reassuring squeeze. She smiled up at her husband, thrilled she and their children could attend this New Testament dedication with him. He had been to several in the last few years, but this was the first for the rest of the Kelceys. As prayer partners with the Tatums, the family had a vested interest in the Yabeja.

Dani knew Keith had been honored to pilot the flights bringing in the boxes of precious New Testaments and visitors for today's festivities. *Thank You, God, for the safety You've given, not just this weekend, but over the years as we've served You in this country. This is a blessing we don't take for granted.*

She quickly glanced at Anna and Chad two rows ahead, seated with the three Tatum children. Maybe at least one of the five would someday become a translator for another people group in Brazil.

The ceremony continued. A group of children, including Moki's oldest grandchild, sang a medley of Scripture choruses in their language. How sweet their praises were!

Brenda joined Ben on the makeshift platform. "For our many guests, I'll explain in English. We'll call out the names of those Yabeja who have memorized 50 or more Bible verses in order to earn a New Testament. Each one will recite a verse of his or her choice. I'll translate."

Dani smiled at Moki, sitting beside her, when her name was called. Her Yabeja friend rose gracefully and slipped out the row past her daughters and three grandchildren. She quoted Romans 5:8: "But God demonstrates His own love toward us, in that while we were yet sinners, Christ died for us." With a grin, she clasped her New Testament to her chest and returned to the bench. Her daughters reached out to reverently touch the red cover of the special book.

Sasi recited Romans 6:23: "For the wages of sin is death, but the free gift of God is eternal life in Christ Jesus our Lord."

Ben handed him a New Testament. Sasi held it up and, eyes lifted toward the sky, spoke with great emotion.

Ben's voice was husky as he translated, "God of creation, You now speak Yabeja, and we promise to listen. Thank You for this book containing Your words. Help us read, obey it, and tell others about You."

Dani saw other guests wiping tears away. *Lord, thank You for allowing the New Testament to be completed in Yabeja, and for each person who had a part, however great or small, over the years in making it available to this people group. Thank You for those who prayed, gave financially, offered encouragement or training to the Tatums, keyboarded the text, proofread, did the consultant checks, flew people in and out of Yabewa, and all the other tasks that are part of producing a New Testament.*

Bless the reading and hearing of Your Word, even as You have promised to do. Continue to build Your church among the Yabeja. In Jesus' Name, Amen.

Order more copies
of *Sketches NOW*

and obtain a free Hannibal Books catalog
Call: 1-800-747-0738
FAX: 1-972-487-7960
Email: orders@hannibalbooks.com
Write: Hannibal Books
P.O. Box 461592
Garland, Texas 75046-1592
Visit: www.hannibalbooks.com

Number of copies desired _____

Multiply number of copies by $9.95   __X__$9.95_____

Cost of books: $_____

Please add $3 for postage and handling for first book and add 50-cents for each additional book in the order.

Shipping $_____

Texas residents add 8.25 % sales tax $_____

Total order $_____

Mark method of payment:

check enclosed _____

Credit card# _____ exp. date_____

(Visa, MasterCard, Discover, American Express accepted)

Name _____

Address _____

City State, Zip _____

Phone _____ FAX _____

Email _____